laguna cove

also by alyson noël

Art Geeks and Prom Queens
Faking 19

laguna cove

alyson noël

st. martin's griffin

new york

For Ryan and Kelsey Sherman,
in memory of their father, Richard Sherman, 1957–2005

LAGUNA COVE. Copyright © 2006 by Alyson Noël. All rights reserved. Printed in the United States of America. For information, address St. Martin's Press, 175 Fifth Avenue, New York, N.Y. 10010.

www.stmartins.com

ISBN-13: 978-0-312-34869-4
ISBN-10: 0-312-34869-X

10 9 8 7 6

acknowledgments

Thank you to Matthew Shear, Elizabeth Bewley, Jennifer Weis, and Stefanie Lindskog, for getting this project started and seeing it through; to Oleema Miller, for answering my many questions; to my favorite Cola Surf Campers—Tyra Larkin, Imara Larkin, Ryan Sherman, and Kelsey Sherman—who make it look so easy; and, as always, to Sandy Sherman, for absolutely everything.

chapter one

"Excuse me. You're in my seat."

Anne brushed her long blond hair out of her blue eyes and squinted at the man standing next to her. His hair was dark, with the kind of deep side part used to disguise the early stages of baldness, and his charcoal gray suit, light blue shirt, and red tie were all slightly rumpled. Still, he looked vaguely familiar.

"I always book 2A." He gave her a condescending look.

"Oh, sorry. I guess you're right. I'm supposed to be in 2B. I'll move," she said, picking up the letter she'd been writing and grabbing her bag.

"Forget it." He sighed loudly, dropping his briefcase onto the aisle seat. "Just stay. I'll take B."

"Whatever." She rolled her eyes and focused again on her letter, making sure she hunched over it so he couldn't peek. She was in no mood to be messed with by some balding old fart. It was because of old people like him (namely her parents) that she was on this stupid plane in the first place. Did they really think that buying her a first-class ticket would lessen the pain of being dragged away from everything she knew and loved? Like the group of close friends she'd had since childhood, her hard-earned status as captain of the dive team, and Justin, the love of her life whom she'd been dating for the last year and a half? Did they really think they could buy her off with an oversized seat, hot towels, and a choice of six movies?

The plane pushed away from the gate and the flight attendants asked everyone to direct their attention to the safety demonstration on the video screens. But Anne refused to look—there was no way some stupid video could save her from a crash. Thanks to her mom's affair with the senior partner at her law firm, and the bitter divorce that immediately followed her dad's walking in on them, Anne's life as she knew it was completely crashing down around her, and there was nothing she could do to save it.

"Sir, you need to turn off your cell phone immediately."

Anne looked up to see an attendant with her hands placed firmly on her navy-clad hips. She was scowling at Mr. 2B. "Sir, don't make me say it twice."

"Excuse me," he said, putting his hand over the mouthpiece and glaring. "Do you know who I am?"

"Yes, Mr. O'Rourke, I've seen your show. And if you don't turn off your phone right this minute, we will return to the gate so you can disembark and continue your call while we fly to Los Angeles without you." She reached up and smoothed her blond French twist.

Anne watched him snap his phone shut and mumble something under his breath as the attendant walked away. *Oh my God, no wonder he looks familiar.* It was Bob O'Rourke from that news show on FOX. And she was sitting in his favorite seat, and she'd even rolled her eyes at him! But he was kind of a jerk, so she didn't feel too bad about it.

The plane began its runway roll, quickly gaining speed. This was the moment when Anne would normally reach over and hold her dad's hand until the wheels lifted off the tarmac and retreated into the belly. She looked over at Bob O'Rourke, glasses perched on the end of his nose, scowling at a stack of papers in his hand,

and she knew better than to even try. She was on her own now, in more ways than one.

She closed the window shade, fearing she might cry if she glimpsed the diminishing East Coast landscape, then reread her letter. But halfway through, her throat grew hot and tight and her eyes started to sting, so she quickly scribbled at the bottom, telling Justin how much she loved and missed him. Then she folded the letter into a perfect rectangle, stuffed it into an envelope, and shoved it deep inside her purse.

She was just drifting off to sleep when that same attendant came by and asked if they'd like anything to drink. And after listening to the very important Bob O'Rourke grill her about the available wines and their grape origins, Anne was feeling so bad for her she said, "Um, I'll just have a bottle of water. I don't need a glass or anything." Then, determined to ignore the famous jerk beside her, she put on her headphones, extended her footrest, and turned on her in-seat video unit.

On channel 3 they were showing that movie *Blue Crush*, but Anne flipped right past it. No way was she gonna watch a bunch of sun-struck surfer girls talk about the beach and "killer" waves. She'd be forced to live among people like that soon enough, and she was in no rush to get there.

She was down to just a five-hour cushion between her beloved old life and her dreaded new one, and she was determined to make the most of it. The only surfing she planned on doing was channel surfing.

She thought about her last phone call with her dad, and how he sounded so excited when he told her about the house he'd bought. "It's in a private gated community called Laguna Cove, and we're right on a cliff overlooking our very own beach."

"We have our own beach?" she'd asked.

"Well, we have to share it with the neighbors." He laughed.

"Is there a pool?" Anne remembered asking.

"No, honey, there's not. But I think you're really gonna like it here if you just give it a chance."

Easy for him to say, since he's never home much anyway, always away on location, or busy schmoozing with fellow movie execs. And how could she possibly like a place with no pool? Diving was her passion! She'd spent the last three years at her private school earning a reputation as a skilled and fearless competitor. And then, right when she finally makes captain, they yank her and send her to some stupid California beach town that's probably filled with pot-smoking hippie surfers named after flowers. She wasn't being negative, she told herself, just realistic.

The flight attendant reappeared with a bottle of water for Anne and a glass of red wine for the jerk in 2B, who was currently missing in action. "I'll just set this here for when he returns," she said.

But by the time they came by with the meals, he still wasn't back.

"Do you know what happened to the person that was sitting here?" Anne asked the male attendant with a deep tan and tightly cropped, bleached blond hair. "I think his name was Bob O'Rourke?"

"He moved to 5C. Looks like you're on your own. Do you need more wine?" he asked, motioning toward the untouched glass.

"Um, no. Maybe in a little while."

Then, the second he was gone, Anne craned her head around and peered down the aisle at 5C. Sure enough, there was Bob O'Rourke, napkin tucked into his collar, smug nose buried deep into his wineglass. Carefully picking up the wine next to her, she placed it on her own tray. Then she looked around nervously, to see if anyone noticed, but nobody seemed to care. Besides, the attendant guy thought it was hers, so it may as well be.

She lifted the glass to her nose and inhaled just like that O'Rourke guy did. Though she wasn't exactly sure what she was supposed to be sniffing for. Was it to see if it's rancid? And what did rancid wine smell like anyway?

She lowered the glass to her lips and sipped cautiously. Sometimes she and her friends drank beer and once, last New Year's, champagne, but this wasn't too bad.

So she took another sip.

And no one seemed to notice she was still four years away from her twenty-first birthday.

Maybe flying first class wasn't so bad after all.

"Miss, Miss. Excuse me, we've landed."

"What?" Anne opened her eyes to find the blond attendant with the French twist kneeling next to her. "Are you feeling all right?" she asked, eyes narrowed with concern.

"Um, yeah. How much longer?"

"We're here."

"What? Oh my God! Okay, just let me get my stuff," Anne said, running her fingers through her tangled, messed-up hair and searching the seat-back pocket for her bottle of water. The inside of her mouth felt like the Mojave Desert.

"Are you sure you're okay?" the attendant asked again.

"Yeah, really I'm fine," Anne assured her, even though she felt the exact opposite of fine with her throbbing head and stinging eyes. *And where is that damn water bottle?*

"Well, we're laying over and our van is waiting, so you really need to hurry." She stood and ran her hands over her tight blue skirt.

"Okay, okay, I'm ready. Do you know where baggage claim is?" Anne asked.

"You can follow us."

Anne stumbled behind the flight crew, listening to their laughter as they made fun of Bob O'Rourke. And even though she had no idea what their lives might really be like, at that exact moment she would have traded places with any one of them, no questions asked. Because at this point just about anyone's life looked better than what she was in for.

Okay, maybe on the surface, moving to Laguna Beach, into a big house with a private beach, didn't sound so bad, but it was all relative to what she was leaving behind.

She shifted her purse to the other shoulder and mentally scolded herself for drinking too much, passing out, and generally wasting the past five hours on the plane. And now she didn't even have time to freshen up, since she knew her dad would be waiting at baggage claim. And even though she didn't have time to look in a mirror, she was willing to bet she wasn't exactly at her best right now.

The blond attendant stopped and turned while the rest of the group continued ahead. "You can take that escalator right over there all the way down to the baggage carousels. Have fun!" she said, turning and rushing to catch up with the rest of the crew.

Anne used the thirty-second escalator ride for some quick damage control. Breath mint? Check. Stila lip gloss? Check. Designer sunglasses? Check. Red wine stains on brand-new vintage-wash two-hundred-dollar jeans? Triple check. Ridiculously expensive wrinkled-up white T-shirt with drool stain dripping down the front? You bet.

God, what she really needed was a toothbrush, a shower, and a decent meal to soak up all the alcohol. But since she hadn't seen her dad for the month he spent getting the house ready, she was banking on the fact that he'd be so excited to see her that he wouldn't notice how she'd boozed it up in first class.

And speaking of Dad, where the hell was he? At six foot three, with a lean build and a head of thick silver hair, it's not like he was hard to miss. But after scanning the crowd she didn't see him anywhere.

Oh, please, don't let him be late, she thought, heading over to the baggage carousel and retrieving her cell phone from the bottom of her purse. But when she flipped it open and tried to turn it on, nothing happened. *Oh, great.* She'd used up her entire battery on the limo ride from her house in Connecticut to the JFK Airport. About thirty seconds were spent saying good-bye to her mom. The rest was saying good-bye to her friends and, of course, Justin.

She sat there with her two oversized bags and wondered what the hell she was supposed to do now. She didn't even know where she lived.

chapter two

"Are you Anne?"

Anne looked up to see a guy with messy longish wavy brown hair wearing a surf logo T-shirt, shredded flip-flops, and dark blue board shorts. He was kind of cute. *If you like that sort of thing,* she thought.

But she was a savvy New Yorker, not some sun-drained local. So she narrowed her eyes and said, "Maybe."

"Cut me some slack, would ya? Traffic on the 405 was a bitch, and if your dad finds out I was late, he'll kill me." He smiled then, exposing a slight gap between his two front teeth. But even though it made him look even cuter, Anne was unmoved. After all, she had a boyfriend. She was no pushover.

"So how do you know my dad?" she asked, folding her arms across her chest and enjoying herself for the first time in too many hours to count.

"He's my boss. I run errands for him and stuff. My name's Jake."

"Are you my new nanny?" She laughed.

Jake shook his head and glanced at the display on his cell phone. "C'mon, dude, I'm in a time crunch."

"Okay," Anne said, standing up and grabbing her bag. "But I'm driving."

"I don't think so," he said, taking her bag and leading her out the door to the parking structure.

"I'm a good driver. I've had my license for almost six months." She narrowed her eyes at him.

"Maybe so, but have you seen your teeth recently? They're all purple. Looks like you've been hittin' it hard on the plane."

"Are you serious?" she asked, panicked.

"See for yourself." He opened the door of the silver Mercedes convertible and flipped down the mirrored visor.

"Oh, God. My dad's gonna *kill* me. Can we stop somewhere so I can brush my teeth?"

"Dude, you need a little more than that. Let's get you a coffee, some aspirin, and a bottle of water. I've got some Visine right here."

Big surprise. "I really appreciate that. But can you do me a favor?" Anne asked, more than a little annoyed with him for insinuating that she was drunk, even though she was.

"Sure, what?"

"Please stop calling me dude. My name is Anne."

"Whatever."

Despite the double-shot venti nonfat latte she practically inhaled, Anne fell right to sleep. It wasn't until Jake nudged her hard in the arm and said, "You're not gonna want to miss this," that she woke up.

"Where are we?" she asked, rubbing her eyes and straightening her T-shirt, which had risen up and twisted around.

"Laguna Beach. This is Laguna Canyon Road, and in just a few minutes you won't believe your eyes."

He was right. They drove through a narrow, twisting road cut right down the center of a canyon and then suddenly came to a halt. Right in front of her was a big gorgeous beach filled with volleyball players, basketball players, sunbathers, and body boarders.

"What beach is that?" she asked, trying to sound only curious and not at all impressed.

"Main Beach."

"It's nice." She shrugged, craning her neck to look back at it, as he turned left onto Pacific Coast Highway.

"You think that's nice, wait 'til you see your beach. That's one of the best benefits of working for your dad. Your beach has awesome waves, and I get to surf there nearly every day."

"I'm not interested in that. I'm into diving," Anne said, gawking at the beautiful coastline in spite of herself.

"That's cool." He nodded. "But you really should try it."

"No thanks," she said, crossing her arms in front of her.

Jake continued down PCH, past huge custom oceanfront homes, and a spectacular, sprawling resort called the Montage. "We're almost there," he said, waving at the uniformed guard and driving through the gate.

"This is where I live? This is Laguna Cove?" Anne asked, unable to keep the excitement out of her voice.

"This is it. See the house on the end? That's yours."

"Oh. My. God." She sat and stared at the large, sprawling home built on the edge of a cliff as Jake parked in the driveway.

"Go ahead," he said. "I'll get your bags."

Anne grabbed her purse and ran for the door, excited to see her dad and check out her new room. But when she tried to open it, the door was locked. So she knocked. But nobody answered. "Dad?" she called, knocking even louder and ringing the bell.

"He's probably not home yet. Here, use the key," Jake said, tossing her a shiny gold key.

"But he'll be home soon, right?" she asked, opening the door to an expansive foyer filled with tropical plants and freshly cut flowers.

"Doubtful. They were having problems on the set, and he said he didn't know if he'd make it home tonight. But I'm sure he'll call you later."

"You mean I'm supposed to stay here *by myself*?" she asked, feeling more than a little panicked.

"Yeah. You can totally party. But if I were you, I'd just lie down and take a nap," Jake said, setting her bags on the travertine-tiled floor.

"Well, where are you going?" she asked, suddenly dreading his leaving. The last thing she wanted was to be left alone in the big unfamiliar house.

"Hittin' the beach. There's six-foot swells out there." He smiled.

"But, don't you have more work to do? You said in the airport that you were on a time crunch." She hated herself for sounding so needy.

"I didn't want to miss the surf. You were my last chore." He shrugged.

"Thanks a lot," she said, rolling her eyes.

"You know what I mean." He turned and headed for the door. "See you around," he called over his shoulder.

"Whatever," she said, standing in the foyer, watching him leave. When the door closed behind him, she was left with nothing but an overwhelming loneliness and complete silence. *I better get used to it,* she thought. Then she grabbed her bags and walked down a long hallway in search of her new bedroom.

chapter three

Ellie weaved her long white-blond hair into a single braid that cascaded all the way down her back, landing just short of her bikini bottoms. She wriggled into her wetsuit and looked at the clock one last time. It was already five forty-five and there was still no sign of them.

Grabbing her surfboard, she headed out, closing the glass sliding door slowly and carefully behind her. The last thing she needed was to wake up her brother, who had come in late the night before, or even worse her dad, who was on her case for just about everything these days.

She made her way down the stairs leading from her house to the beach, and scanned for her friends, hoping they were already out there, but secretly knowing better.

After a few stretches and beach sprints to warm up her tired muscles, she headed into the water, dropped her board, and began paddling out. When she got past the break, she lay resting, with her chin propped against her folded arms, enjoying the mellow sway of the water and the quiet solitude of an empty beach. She loved getting out early and watching the ocean change from a moonlit sparkly sequin to a sun-warmed velvet. But even though she liked having the waves to herself and not having to wait in a never-ending lineup, she still missed the company of her best friends, Lola and Jade.

It had started last spring. The early-morning surf ritual that had bonded them all through elementary, junior high, and well into their freshman and sophomore years of high school began to gradually taper off. First to three times a week, then two, and now, by early September, she was lucky if they surfed together on a random Saturday. And even then, by the time they showed up practically all of Laguna Cove was in the lineup and it took all day just to get a turn.

But Jade and Lola didn't seem to care. Suddenly, they were content to just lie on their towels reading fashion magazines and checking out all the guys, just like all the other beach Barbies they used to make fun of, and Ellie just didn't get it. For one thing, the guys they were looking at were the same old totally immature, unfocused bros they'd known since grade school. And Ellie knew for a fact that not one of them was worth talking about, much less missing waves for.

Well, except for Chris, who was not only amazingly cute, with his aqua-blue eyes (the same color as the Fiji waters on a cloudless day), tanned skin, and shaggy, sun-streaked hair that was constantly falling into his eyes, but also incredibly smart (he was in all the same advanced-placement classes as she) and an accomplished surfer, maybe even the best in Laguna Cove (well, after her older brother, Dean).

But nobody knew how she felt about Chris—not Jade, not Lola, and definitely *not Chris*! To him, they were just good buds who went way back, and that's the way it would have to stay. Ellie couldn't afford to waste time obsessing over some guy. She had to stay focused on the important things, like maintaining her perfect 4.0 GPA, her position as Surf Club president, and taking first at the upcoming San Onofre Surf Fest competition so she could get noticed by the sponsors she'd been dreaming of for too many years to count.

With her five-foot-nine, slim, toned frame and long blond hair pulled back into its usual braid or ponytail, exposing her perfect face, there was something so graceful and delicate about her, people often assumed she was a model or ballerina—that is, until they saw her surf. In the ocean, she was a strong and fearless competitor who could carve up the face of a wave with both elegance and aggression.

Guys also came easy to Ellie, always drawn first by her looks, then later by her brains and talent. She had a handful of good guy friends she could always count on as a last-minute prom date or emergency flat-tire fixer. But she never allowed any of these friendships to go further than a quick peck on the cheek or, even more likely, a brief hug. That she could have pretty much any guy she wanted was merely a fact that didn't mean much to her. Especially since she only wanted one.

But even Chris, awesome as he was, could not get in the way of her dreams. She had a lot to live up to, and it was like her dad always said: "Go after your goals with absolute tunnel vision!" "Allow nothing to get in your way!" "You have to name it before you can claim it!"

Okay, the last may have been Dr. Phil. But whatever. The bottom line was she couldn't allow herself to get distracted. *No matter what.*

She scanned the empty beach, looking for her friends even though she knew they wouldn't show; then, feeling the water beginning to rise and swell beneath her, she started paddling, jumping up on her board with the strength and assurance of someone more comfortable in the ocean than anywhere else. But as always, on her first wave of the day (especially when no one was watching), there were no fancy tricks, no special maneuvers to impress the judges. It was just Ellie, her board, and the ocean all blending in harmony for that one perfect moment. She allowed herself one soul surf a day, but she refused to admit it was always her favorite.

After several decent waves, she checked the tide watch her dad had bought her for Christmas last year and realized she barely had time for one more before she had to head back home, change, and meet her trainer for her two-hour gym workout.

Jumping up on her board, she sensed that this last wave would be the best of the day, as she expertly cranked it around, catching the lip and slicing through the cool, green curl. *If this was the Surf Fest, those sponsors would be double-checking my name right about now,* she thought.

But just as she was going for a really big finish, she spotted another surfer paddling out. Sun-streaked hair, tanned skin, perfect body, and even though she couldn't exactly see them from this distance, she knew the eyes were clear, like blue topaz. And just as she was thinking about those eyes, she lost focus, wiped out, and swallowed salt water right in front of him.

"You okay?" Chris called, just before duck-diving under a wave.

But by the time he resurfaced, she'd already untangled the seaweed from around her legs and retrieved her board, as though nothing had happened. Giving him a casual over-the-shoulder wave, she headed toward the cliff stairs, glad that her back was now to him so he couldn't see that her face was bright red with humiliation, embarrassment, and anger at her own lack of focus.

She opened the little gate that led to the limestone terrace and leaned her board against the low fence. Reaching back to unzip her wetsuit, she looked up and saw her father sitting on a lounge chair by the Jacuzzi, drinking an orange juice.

Oh, great. How long has he been there? she wondered.

"Hey, Dad," she said, casually squeezing salt water from her braid and hoping he hadn't seen her wipe out.

"That's quite a spill you took out there," he said, eyeing her carefully.

"It wasn't that bad, really." She grabbed a towel and headed for the sliding glass doors that led to the living room, hoping he wouldn't follow.

"Tell that to the judges," he said, right behind her now.

"Well, did you happen to see any of the waves I had before that?" she asked, trying to sound neutral so he wouldn't know how upset she was by his criticism. She wiggled out of her wetsuit and hung it on a hook by the door. "Because some of them were really good." She turned to face him briefly, taking in his towering six-foot-four frame, the hair that despite the slight thinning was still as blond as hers, the tanned face, and the deep lines that fanned away from his clear green eyes that were also just like hers.

"All of them have got to be good, Ellie, not just some of them. You think your brother won NSSA by one or two merely decent waves?"

Ellie reached for the door handle and rolled her eyes. But her back was toward him, so it's not like he could see it.

"And don't roll your eyes at me. I can see your reflection in the window, you know."

Leave it to my dad to find a maid that does windows! "Okay, so I slipped a little. Trust me, it's no big deal. I'll get it straight before the contest, so you don't have to worry," she said, hurrying up the stairs to her room, where she could finally escape his never-ending scrutiny.

"Ellie?"

Jeez, what now? she thought. She was just outside her door, *so close to freedom.*

"This is for you." He handed her his platinum credit card. "Stop by the mall later and get yourself whatever you need for school tomorrow."

Taking the card, she looked at him, immediately feeling guilty for everything she'd just been thinking. But it was always like that. He'd pile on the pressure to the point where she was just about to scream, then quickly follow it up by an act of extreme kindness or generosity. She knew he meant well, but sometimes he really got on her nerves.

chapter four

Anne woke to the sound of a persistent high-pitched ringing. Assuming it was there to accompany the incessant drumming in her head (it was beginning to sound like a really bad garage band in there), she lay in her new bed with her eyes shut tight, promising to whoever might be in charge of these things that if they would just put an end to the incessant pounding, the cotton mouth, and the nausea, then she would never, ever drink red wine (or anything else, for that matter) again.

Ever!

Well, at least not until her twenty-first birthday.

Really.

She wasn't just saying that.

When the ringing abruptly stopped, her eyes popped open. *Could it be?* But when it resumed a moment later, she realized it was the phone, not her head, that was making all that racket.

Tossing the covers aside, she stumbled out of bed, wondering where the phone was located. In her old room in Connecticut, she'd had a cordless with her own private number, a cell phone with a different number, a laptop, two e-mail addresses, and a BlackBerry that they could all be forwarded to. And it was all within easy reach of her big, comfortable canopy bed. Communi-

cation with everyone who mattered had always been right at her
fingertips.

But here, in her dad's strange new digs, she didn't even know
where to start. Since she had fallen asleep not long after finding
her room the day before, the rest of the house had so far remained
a mystery. Sprinting out of her room, she headed down the hall
and toward the kitchen, partly because it seemed like the logical
place to start, and partly because it was the only other room she
was familiar with.

"Hello?" she said, picking up the receiver of a brand-new silver-
colored phone designed to look retro, but with all the modern
conveniences.

"Did I wake you?" her dad asked from God-knows-where.

"Kind of. Where are you?" She settled onto a teakwood stool at
a long, narrow table, the kind design magazines always refer to as
a "breakfast bar."

"Still on set. Sorry I wasn't there to greet you yesterday. Things
got a little hectic around here. But I should be back by tonight,"
he said, not sounding very convincing.

Should be? "Oh, okay," she said, feeling completely annoyed
with him, yet cringing at the high-pitched whininess in her own
voice.

"See you then?" he asked, obviously in a hurry to hang up.

"Dad, wait. What exactly am I supposed to do here? I mean, I
feel kind of stranded," she said, looking around the unfamiliar
kitchen, feeling like she'd broken into her own house.

"Call Jake if you need anything. His number is on the pad next
to the phone. Or ask Christina; she should be there by noon."

Christina? Jeez, he was freshly divorced, new to the neighborhood, and he already had a girlfriend? What was with her parents? The way they played musical partners, they were worse than
the kids at school!

She shook her head and rolled her eyes, but it only intensified the throbbing. "Dad, do you think you could . . . ?" She stopped, noticing the absolute silence on the other end. *Oh my God, did he already hang up?* "Hello? *Hello?*" she said, staring at the receiver. He was gone. Just like that. No good-bye, nothing. *How's that for a warm welcome?* she thought, slamming down the phone.

Hopping off the stool, she opened the fridge and peered inside, searching for something to cure what appeared to be her very first (and definitely last) hangover. She grabbed a carton of soy milk and swigged straight from the container. But she didn't get as far as the swallowing part before running straight to the sink where she gagged and spit and rinsed her mouth with tap water until that thick, nasty soy taste was no more than a bad memory. *Gag.* Was her dad turning into some kind of California hippie health freak? Or was it Christina's fault that the fridge was full of weirdo organic stuff she wasn't used to?

Anne glanced at the clock on the stove. Another hour until Christina would be guest-starring in what would surely be her most challenging role to date: that of eager new companion to handsome, newly single dad and his hung over, sulky, resentful (but ultimately well-meaning) daughter.

Anne had a tendency to view her life in movie terms, as though all moments were taking place in front of a live studio audience, and lately there had been no shortage of big, dramatic moments. She always assumed it was just a natural side effect of having a big Hollywood exec for a dad, but lately she wondered if it wasn't just plain weird.

She grabbed a bottle of water from the fridge and wondered what the Ingenue, a.k.a. Christina, would look like. Let's see, her dad was so upset with her mom these days, it was safe to assume he'd go for the complete opposite. Like maybe a Kate Hudson meets Meg Ryan type—the kind of sexy/wholesome L.A. hybrid that can make an entire career out of lame, formulaic romantic comedies.

Though, it was kind of creepy picturing her dad with someone like that. Someone so different from her mom's own look of sharp, sleek, elegant New York City attorney who ultimately cheats on her husband and destroys her family. Yeah, her mom was definitely more the femme fatale, film noir type.

But Anne didn't like thinking about her mom any more than her dad probably did. It was because of *her* that they were both living here in this dreadful, sunny place. And even though Anne knew firsthand just how much it sucked to be constantly ignored by her work-obsessed dad, the truth was *she* was dealing with it, so why couldn't her mom? After all, *they* were the adults! *They* were the ones who took the vows!

They were also the ones who taught her all about "honoring your commitments," and all kinds of other values that they themselves apparently didn't practice. It's like, ever since the divorce it seemed they'd conveniently forgotten all the lessons they'd taught her, and the line between parent and child had become extremely blurred.

Grabbing a banana from a silver wire basket, she headed out the sliding doors and onto the flagstone terrace overlooking the beach. She walked to the railing and leaned against it, peeling the banana skin and squinting into the sun toward the ocean. There were five, maybe six surfers all lined up, floating on their boards, laughing and joking while they waited their turn.

She finished her banana and left the peel lying on the railing, then walked down the stairs and sat on the very last one so she could get a closer look. The beach was a perfect little cove, with light, clean sand dotted with beachgoers' umbrellas, two wooden lifeguard stands, and what looked to be a much-used volleyball net at the far end. And even though she was determined not to like it here, the fact was she couldn't believe this beach was actually hers. Well, not hers exactly—there were plenty of other families in the neighborhood. But still, it was hers in the way that it was right at her fingertips, right at the bottom of her stairs.

She watched the surfers catching waves, one after another, some gliding gracefully to shore, some wiping out and pounding sand. But as much as she loved the water and loved to swim, she was way more comfortable in a pool than the ocean. It was the smell of chlorine, not salt water, that got her excited. She really hoped her new school would have a diving team.

Stretching her long legs out in front of her, she wondered if it was weird to be sitting outside in the hot sun in her pajamas. But since her pj's consisted of a thick white ribbed tank top and royal-blue boxers with white flowers, she decided they didn't look so out of place. Closing her eyes, she tilted her head back, enjoying the way the sun warmed her face.

"Hey, did you sleep it off?"

Anne opened her eyes to find that annoying Jake guy standing right in front of her—hair stringy with salt water, lips cracked and chapped, beat-up surfboard held under his arm. Something about his ultra-cool, laid-back way totally got on her nerves. He was *sooo* California. It's like he came right out of central casting or something.

"I don't know what you're referring to, but I slept well, thank you," she said, looking right at him and hating the way she just sounded like the most uptight bitch on the planet.

But Jake was unfazed. "Awesome. Well, your dad wanted me to check in on you. Do you need anything?" he asked, flipping his wet hair a couple times and spraying Anne with water.

"Yeah. He just called; he wants you to leave me the keys," she said, holding his gaze without blinking.

"Oh, yeah? What keys?" he asked, smiling.

"The keys to the Mercedes. I have errands to run." She crossed her legs and pointed her toes toward the sand.

"Nice try." He laughed.

Anne shrugged and looked down at her feet. She knew better than to push it; she'd get her hands on those keys eventually.

"Hey, nice ride, dude. I saw you catch some air out there."

What the heck is he talking about now? Anne thought, looking up to find this incredibly cute guy standing right in front of her, next to Jake.

"It was okay. It's a little mushy out there," he said, looking at Jake and then smiling at her.

Gorgeous turquoise eyes, straight white teeth, tight abs. . . . Uh, hello? You have a boyfriend, she thought, scolding herself. Just because she moved three thousand miles away didn't mean it was over with Justin. Just two days ago they'd promised they'd wait for each other, and now some cute local appears and she starts drooling like one of Pavlov's dogs.

"This is Anne," Jake said, nodding in her direction.

"Hey, I'm Chris." The gorgeous guy smiled and extended his hand.

Anne shook his hand briefly, then quickly pulled away.

"Do you surf?" asked Chris, still smiling.

"No," Anne said, shaking her head and looking away. *God, what's with him? It's like someone told him he has nice teeth so now he smiles all the time.*

"That's too bad," he said.

"Whatever." She shrugged, knowing she was acting like a defensive brat, but not really willing to stop.

"What school are you going to?" he asked, seemingly unfazed by her bad attitude.

"Laguna Beach."

"Me too. What year are you?"

"Junior," she said, still looking at the water and not at him.

"Me too. So I guess I'll see you Monday then," he said, *still smiling.*

"I guess." Anne stood and turned to head back up the stairs. *God, is everyone here like this? Tanned and happy and smiley and friendly and gorgeous?* She sincerely hoped not.

And then she heard Jake say, "I'll stop by later to see if you need anything."

Anne turned, looking briefly at Chris and then at Jake. "I don't need a baby-sitter. I don't need anything," she said. Then she turned and walked back up the stairs before either one of them could respond.

chapter five

"Lola? Is that all you're having?"

"*Sí, Abuela.* I'm fine." Lola looked across the table and smiled patiently at her grandmother. This was all part of the normal breakfast routine Lola had come to expect ever since her grandmother had come to live with them. And it was so predictable she was often tempted to walk into the kitchen, slap a tape recorder right next to her cereal bowl, lift her spoon, and push play.

"Let me make you some eggs and toast," her grandmother offered, smoothing her shapeless floral cotton dress as she rose from her seat.

"*Abuela,* please. I don't want eggs. Besides, Ellie will be here any second," she said, glancing at the clock and hurriedly finishing her Cheerios.

"Nonsense. You hardly ate any breakfast. You're too thin," she said, eyeing her tiny granddaughter with disapproval. "You'll never find a husband looking like that."

"Well, considering that I'm still in high school, that's probably a good thing," Lola said, getting up from the table and placing her bowl in the dishwasher.

Abuela was her father's mother, who, after *Abuelo*'s passing just over a year ago, had reluctantly moved from Mexico City to live with them, bringing nothing more than two trunks full of cotton housedresses and all of her old-school beliefs—actively disapproving of just about everything in her new life in Laguna Beach. If it was up to her, Lola's mother would stay home all day preparing meals for her family, and Lola would be twenty pounds heavier, dressed in her first communion garb, and engaged to be married to a nice Mexican boy from a good family the day after her high-school graduation. The only thing *Abuela* seemed to approve of was her son. Lola's father could do no wrong.

"Lola, don't forget you have cotillion practice this evening," her mother said, striding into the room and bending down to briefly kiss *Abuela* on the cheek.

What a contrast they are, Lola thought, looking at *Abuela*'s short, round body clothed in one of her numerous tent dresses and her mother's tall, sleek, elegant form perfectly turned out in one of her designer suits. *I got Grandma's lack of height and major stubbornness, but thankfully my mom's slim build and straight dark hair,* Lola thought. It's her eyes that were like her dad's, shiny, dark, and deep like onyx.

"Mom, I'll try to make it but I can't promise anything. It's the first day of school and all."

"No 'and all,' Lola. Say 'It's the first day of school,' period."

"Yeah, yeah," Lola said, bending down to kiss *Abuela* just as Ellie pulled into the driveway and honked.

"Is that Ellie?" *Abuela* asked.

"*Sí, Abuela.* I'll see you later," she said, grabbing her bag and heading toward the door.

"Can you please inform her, once again, that it is impolite to honk?"

Lola shook her head, put her hands on her hips, and breathed an exasperated sigh. "No, I cannot. Because she's doing me a big favor by driving me to school. And if your son and daughter-in-law would just buy me a car, once and for all, then I could drive myself and you'd be spared the honking," she said.

"What did she say?" *Abuela* asked, looking to her daughter-in-law for help with the translation. But Lola knew better. *Abuela's* perfect English always seemed to fail in the most convenient moments.

Lola's mom shook her head. "Get your grades up, and we'll talk."

"Yeah, yeah." Lola slung her book bag over her shoulder and walked out the door. She'd gotten only one B in an all-A lineup, but that had been enough for her overly strict parents to refuse her a car. True, the deal had been all A's gets the wheels, *but still.* Lola had done her very best, and just because she got four wrong answers on that chemistry test (*Chemistry!* It's not like she wanted to be a scientist!), she was relegated to another semester of being chauffeured to school by her friends. And it was really getting old.

Usually she didn't mind being driven everywhere, but in the last few weeks she'd found a very good reason to get her own car and a little more privacy. So now she was very motivated to get straight A's and not screw up.

"Hey, El." Lola opened the passenger door of Ellie's new jet-black Mini Cooper convertible and plopped down onto the seat next to her. "Are we picking up Jade?"

"No, she's meeting us there," Ellie said, turning onto the street as Lola released her long, dark hair from its tight ponytail and removed her high-necked sweater to reveal the tight little T-shirt underneath. Her family may call her Lola, but her friends, knowing the real Lola was only revealed when her parents weren't looking, often called her Lolita. "You missed some good waves this morning," Ellie said, taking in her friend's transformation.

"I just can't wake up that early anymore. I don't know how you do it." Lola applied shiny peach lip gloss while checking out the cute guy in the black Jeep Wrangler right next to them.

"Discipline, that's how I do it."

"Yeah, discipline and no social life," Lola said, smiling at the guy with her newly shiny lips.

"Excuse me? I have a social life. For your information, I'm planning on yet another year as your class president, yearbook committee, Surf Club president . . ."

"I mean a social life that takes place after the final bell," Lola said, interrupting her friend and laughing.

"Not all of us stay out all night, Lolita!" Ellie said, looking over at her and smiling. "Oh my God, are you flirting with that guy?" She stared in disbelief.

"Maybe."

"Oh my God, he's like, *old*."

"No, he's not. He's probably twenty-five, twenty-six tops. And he's *sooo* cute," Lola said, rolling down her window to get a better look.

"He's probably married, with three kids, and a wife at home who's gonna come after you when she hears about this," Ellie said, half joking and half worrying it could be true.

"I never flirt if they're wearing a ring, or a girlfriend is present. I'm very old-fashioned that way," Lola said, all her attention focused on the cute driver of the black Jeep.

"Well, could you please stop? The last thing I need is to have some pervert following us to school," Ellie said, sounding more than a little uptight.

"Relax; it's over. He's turning right. Well, it was good while it lasted," Lola said, waving at the back of his Jeep. "Hey, can you drop me off at the corner up there?"

"What? Why?" Ellie looked at her.

"I'm meeting someone," she said, running her fingers through her long dark hair and double-checking her lip gloss in the mirrored visor.

"Do you want me to wait for you?" Ellie asked, slowing to a stop.

"No. I'll see you at school."

Ellie gave her a suspicious look.

"Really, I'll catch up with you later."

"If I didn't know you better, I'd swear you were either a drug dealer or a special agent."

"Who, me?" Lola asked, grabbing her books and slipping quickly out of the car.

chapter six

Jade saw Ellie the second she pulled into the parking lot. And she would have run over to greet her friend, if that hadn't happened to be the exact same moment that Ben had picked her up, thrown her over his shoulder, and headed toward the quad with her.

"Ellie!" Jade called, hanging over Ben's shoulder, laughing and waving, determined to ignore the "Ellie look" her friend had plastered across her face. Jade was all too familiar with that look, as Ellie seemed to direct it at her more and more these days. It said something like, *I'm disappointed in you, but I still love you, even though I worry about you.* But Jade forgave her. Because Jade forgave just about everyone. After all, not everyone subscribed to her "live and let live" credo, *especially* Ellie.

Still, they'd been friends forever. Long before pancreatic cancer took Ellie's mother's life. Long before Ellie's dad, angry and wracked with grief, began putting enormous pressure on her to succeed at absolutely everything. Long before Ellie, suffering from the huge emotional void left by her mother's passing, started putting even more pressure on herself than her dad did.

Jade understood just how much Ellie had changed in the past few years. And Jade worried about Ellie just as much as she knew

Ellie worried about her. But she loved Ellie enough to tolerate her constant disapproval. Well, most of the time.

"Ellie!" Jade yelled again, kicking Ben in the ribs until he finally set her down. "Great sweater," she said, her smile exposing that one slightly crooked front tooth that looked like it was determined to overlap the next one, as she pushed her long, dark, out-of-control ringlets away from her face.

"Thanks," Ellie said, rubbing her hand absently over the new kelly-green cashmere cardigan she'd bought the day before with her dad's credit card. "Who is that guy?" Ellie asked, watching Ben joke with some people a few feet away.

"Ben Parker. He just transferred from Sage Hill," Jade said, wishing her friend would lighten up just a little.

"Why would someone transfer here from there? Did he mess up?"

"No. His parents split and his mom couldn't afford the tuition anymore. Cut him some slack, okay? He's a really nice guy."

"How do you know him?" Ellie asked.

"I met him last week at that barbecue at Salt Creek Beach. The one you didn't go to."

"Is he one of the ones that got busted for drinking?"

Jade shook her head. "Listen, I'm taking the Fifth on that one, because it has nothing to do with me, *or you*." Jade was probably the only girl in school that took those yearly anti-gossip vows seriously. "Now come on, our old friend Chris is right over there and I swear he's even yummier this year than last, if you can believe it. And I don't even go for blonds." She laughed.

"I've already seen him," Ellie said, trying to sound casual, but failing miserably.

"Oh, yeah? Do tell."

"I saw him surfing yesterday morning. When I was waiting for you, I might add." Ellie looked at her.

"About that. Listen, I know you're probably really disappointed in me, but it was the last day of summer so I slept in and I just can't apologize for that because getting up at o' dark thirty just goes against the laws of nature." She smiled. "So where's Lola?"

"I dropped Lolita off on the corner. Apparently she had a date." Ellie couldn't refrain from rolling her eyes

But Jade had the opposite opinion. "Wow, talk about good time management! Leave it to Lolita to sneak a date in right before the school day has even begun. Oh, how I do admire that girl. Now come on, El, let's go drool over Chris," Jade said, smiling and pulling Ellie in his direction.

But Ellie was having none of it. "I can't. I need to stop by the office," she said.

"What for? It's the first day! What meeting could you possibly have already lined up?" Jade stared at her friend, eyes narrowed, arms folded across her chest. She knew Ellie was lying.

"I need to drop off some papers. But I'll see you at break, okay?"

"Fine. Your loss," Jade said, watching Ellie head toward the office on some sad, made-up mission. *Anything to avoid Chris,* she thought, knowing that she was the only one who knew the truth about Ellie and Chris. Heck, she probably knew it even better than Ellie did, since Ellie was a master at self-deception.

Jade, Ellie, Lola, and Chris went way back. Jade was the first to arrive in Laguna Cove *and,* as she liked to point out, was the only *true* native, having actually been born at home, under the watchful eyes of the midwife, her dad, her two older sisters Ruby and Sapphire, her worried and disapproving grandparents (who begged their daughter to come to her senses and go to a nice, sterile hospital with real doctors and nurses), and, of course, her mother.

But it was because of those very same disapproving grandparents that Jade got to live there in the first place. Jade's mother had come from a wealthy family who did not approve of Jade's father. Their daughter was beautiful and smart and had numerous doctors and lawyers to choose from. So why would she marry an artist? What future was there in that?

But marry they did, flying off to Hawaii the day after college graduation. And by the time they returned, her parents—resigned to the situation—had presented them with their summer home as a wedding gift. It was the least they could do to ensure their future grandkids would be raised properly, and not in some artists' commune or small apartment in Costa Mesa, like they feared.

And now, after several years of moderate success, the demand for her father's paintings had slumped. And with her grandparents now deceased and their debts spiking as her mother's trust fund quickly dwindled, the "ecologically correct" home remodeling that they'd been enduring for the past year was put on indefinite hold, making certain areas of the house resemble an abandoned construction site.

But Jade wasn't bothered. It was easy enough to step around the unfinished areas, and if they all had to share the same bathroom, well, so what? She knew her dad would succeed again, it was just a matter of time. Besides, she was used to living in chaos; since she had grown up with two older sisters and very social parents who believed in an open door policy, there were always all kinds of people drifting in and out of her life. You never knew who you'd find sleeping on the couch on a Sunday morning, and Jade always assumed that's how she became so accepting. She had learned early on that if you just looked hard enough, you'd see that even the most annoying person had something good in them.

By the time she was old enough to walk she was building sand castles on the beach with Ellie, and it was the two of them that had taught Lola how to dive under waves when she first moved to Laguna Cove from Mexico City when she was eight. By the time they were in fourth grade Chris was on the scene, and sharing after-school jaunts to the beach and a love of surfing, he easily became the fourth in their tight little group.

In junior high they were able to maintain their easy, casual friendship, not caring if Chris saw them in their pajamas, or with their faces covered in zit cream. But by ninth grade things started to change. They were all still friends, but it was almost like Chris had shown up that first day of high school suddenly looking like someone who, they all agreed, was really quite gorgeous. They knew him too well to ever think of him *like that,* but just because they felt that way didn't mean anyone else did, and before they knew it flocks of girls were trying to befriend them just to get to Chris. And Jade, Ellie, and Lola were forced to watch as he slowly pulled away from them, drifting from the novelty of one new girl-friend to another (usually a blonde, sometimes smart, but not al-ways nice), until they hardly said more than a quick "hey" to each other as they passed in the halls.

Everyone seemed to get over it and move on, except for Ellie, who one night, after having a few sips of her very first beer (Jade was positive of this; Ellie gave new meaning to the term "straight-laced"), turned to Jade and confided her feelings for Chris with an emotional intensity Jade had never seen in her, much less guessed at. Then, just as Ellie was wiping her nose with the hem of the sweatshirt Jade had spontaneously thrust at her, she clapped her hand over her mouth and bolted straight for the bushes, where she vomited half a bottle of Corona Light. And the subject was never mentioned again.

It saddened Jade to know that Ellie couldn't admit her true feel-ings. Because the truth was, Ellie and Chris would be perfect to-gether. It's like they were *meant* for each other. They were both gorgeous, both focused, both academic whiz kids, both awesome surfers—not to mention that for the past year Chris hadn't really dated anyone. And it seemed like he was starting to come around a little more again

Jade loved a good project—especially when it involved helping someone. And if nothing else happened this semester, she was de-termined to see to it that Chris and Ellie finally got together.

chapter seven

Anne stood in front of her full-length mirror, contemplating. If this were the first day of school in Connecticut, she would be dressed in her usual school uniform of white blouse, plaid skirt, and navy blazer, and she would've been out the door by now, anxious to see her friends and catch up on everything that had happened over the summer.

But Laguna Beach was like another planet compared to Greenwich, and not only did she not have any friends to meet up with, but she had no idea what the "unofficial" school uniform was. Because even though Laguna Beach High was a public school with an open dress code policy, there was still a social dress code that everyone adhered to. All schools were the same in that way. They all had an understood rule of what was acceptable and cool versus what would immediately tag you as a total dork and a complete outsider.

Her goal was simple—don't try to make a fashion statement, just blend in. But in order to blend you had to know the code, and Anne was completely clueless. The only people she knew here were her dad, who called daily but had yet to put in an appearance (it was getting to the point where Anne wondered if her parents hadn't just divorced each other, but also her); Jake, who lived in nothing but board shorts and seemed to have a permanent surfboard leash attached to his ankle; and Christina, who turned out *not* to be her dad's girlfriend, like she'd thought, but instead his housekeeper, who had a very limited command of English and didn't seem overly interested in fashion.

But maybe that isn't fair, Anne thought, *because who gets dressed up to scrub a toilet and mop a floor?*

Anne opened her door a crack and called out, "Christina?"

"*Sí?*" Anne could hear her hurrying down the hall.

"Hi. I mean, um, *buenos días.*" God, she'd taken two years of Spanish and where had it gotten her? "Is this okay?" she asked, pointing at her outfit and shrugging her shoulders up and down dramatically, hoping Christina would understand that she was asking a question.

"*Sí. Muy bonita.*" She nodded, smiling.

"*Bonita?* That's good, right?" Anne asked, straining to recall some basic vocabulary.

"*Sí,* very beautiful." Christina smiled and nodded, before heading back down the hall so she could get back to doing the dishes and watching her *novelas* on the small TV in the kitchen.

Anne looked in the mirror skeptically. Christina seemed sincere, but then again her dad was paying her. Was it possible she was just being nice? Was it possible she thought Anne was needy, spoiled, insecure, and ridiculous?

Yes, it was definitely possible.

"Hey! Aren't you ready, yet?" Jake asked, knocking on her door.

"Just a minute," Anne yelled. *Ugh, Jake again.* She was so over him. And why did he have to take her to school anyway? *He should just leave me the keys and go send faxes and run errands or whatever he does for my dad,* she thought.

"You're seriously running late. And FYI, the big dogs at Laguna

Beach High don't go for that. And I should know. I was suspended twice," he yelled through the thick wood of her bedroom door, as though he was actually proud of that.

"Fine, I'm ready," she said, throwing her door open and facing him.

"Is that what you're wearing?" he asked, eyes going wide.

"Yeah? Why? What's wrong with it?" The way he was looking at her made her feel completely paranoid.

"Nothing. You look . . . really nice," he said, his face turning slightly red as he quickly turned and headed for the front door.

"I think it's time you let *me* drive," Anne said, reaching for the keys in his hand.

"Not this again." He shook his head and switched the keys to his other hand.

"Come on, Jake. How else am I gonna learn my way around?" she whined.

"By paying attention. Now come on. Get in. We've got fifteen minutes before your bell rings."

Jake pulled up to the curb in front of the administration office. "Okay, just go into the office there, introduce yourself, and they'll tell you where to go next."

"Gee thanks, Mom," she said, smiling and shutting the door between them.

"Call if you need anything. Otherwise I'll see ya around three fifteen," he told her as he put the convertible top down.

"Aren't you gonna give me my lunch money?" she asked.

"Do you need some?" He reached into his pocket.

She shook her head and laughed. "I was joking. See ya later," she called over her shoulder and headed toward the office, trying to look confident on the outside so no one would know about all the trembling on the inside.

• • •

The office lady was pretty nice, and after get-
ting detailed directions to her classroom Anne was walking across
campus when she could have sworn she heard someone call her
name. *I'm losing it,* she thought. *No one here knows me.*

"Anne! Over here."

No, that was definitely someone calling her. She turned to see
some total hottie smiling and waving. And after standing and
squinting at him for just a little too long, she realized it was that
surfer guy, Chris, who was talking to Jake on the beach yesterday.

"Come 'ere," he called.

Anne shyly approached him, noticing he was surrounded by a
bunch of people, all dressed far more casually than her in surf
tees, shorts, and flip-flops (the guys), or camis with minis or low-
cut jeans and flip-flops (the girls). By the time she was standing in
front of them in her dark-rinse designer jeans, black stiletto
boots, and form-fitting, jewel-neck black cashmere sweater, she
felt completely out of place and like a major dork. She'd gotten it
so wrong she looked more like a teacher than a student.

"I almost didn't recognize you without your surfboard," she
said, smiling and trying to sound confident and breezy, despite
the fact that everyone was staring at her.

Chris smiled and put his arm loosely around her, like they'd
been friends forever. Normally Anne would be creeped out by
that. She couldn't stand overly confident guys who knew they
were hot and just assumed all girls wanted to be wrapped not just
in their presence, but also in their arms. But it was different with
Chris. She could tell he was just genuinely nice, and somehow his
arm felt oddly comforting.

"You guys, this is Anne. She just moved here from New York,"
he said.

"Connecticut," she corrected him.

"The East Coast." He laughed. "So, this is Jade, Ben, Hunter, and that's Ellie over there." He pointed to a very pretty blond girl, who had just walked up.

"Who's this?" Ellie asked, stopping to look Anne over from head to toe.

"Anne. She's new."

Ellie smiled but Anne noticed it was only perfunctory. And there was a big difference between being polite and being real.

"How do you two know each other?" Ellie asked, still staring at Anne.

"We met on the beach. She's a friend of Jake's," he said.

Anne just stood there, wishing he hadn't said she was "friends" with Jake. She really thought of him more as a nuisance.

"Oh, Jake's so cool. How do you know him?" asked the girl Anne thought was named Jade.

"He works for my dad." She shrugged.

"Oh my God, then you live right down the street from Ellie, Chris, and our friend Lola, who's not here yet. Oh, and right down the hill from me!"

Anne looked at Jade and her huge friendly smile. She seemed to be truly happy about that. Then Anne looked over at Ellie, who seemed a lot less so.

"Do you surf?" Ellie asked, shifting her backpack to her other shoulder and giving Anne a look she couldn't quite define.

"No. Actually I'm really into diving. I'd just made captain at my old school, but then—" She stopped. Oh God, what was she doing? Nobody wanted to hear her sob story. "Anyway, I've gone boogie boarding, but no, I've never surfed." She shrugged.

"*Body* boarding. No one says 'boogie.' And it's not really the same thing, is it?" Ellie said, rolling her eyes.

Anne looked down at the ground, noticing how everyone had

gone quiet. *Great, just five minutes into the school day, and it's already a disaster.* She felt completely homesick.

"What class do you have now?" Jade asked, breaking the silence.

"Um, AP English," Anne said, looking at her schedule for confirmation, even though she'd already memorized it.

"Ellie has AP English, too. Maybe she could show you where it is?" Jade said, giving Ellie a meaningful look.

"Sorry. I would walk you, but I have to stop somewhere first and I don't want to make you late," Ellie said, looking first at Jade and then at Anne.

"I'll show you," Chris volunteered.

"That's okay; I'm sure I can find it," Anne said, turning to leave, anxious to get away from Ellie.

"No worries. It's on my way," he insisted.

And even though he didn't slip his arm around her, by the look on Ellie's face, he may as well have.

chapter eight

Ellie stood in front of the bathroom mirror, gripping the sink and staring at her reflection. What was wrong with her? She'd acted so awful toward that new girl, but even when she'd realized how evil she was being, she'd been completely unable to stop. It's like there was this little voice in her head whispering, "Lighten up!" and "What's your problem?" But somehow she managed to ignore it, forging right ahead with the dirty looks, snide comments, and just overall brattiness.

Turning on the faucet, she let the cool water fall against her up-turned wrists, closing her eyes until she began to feel herself grow calmer. She remembered when her mom had taught her this trick years ago. It was right after she was diagnosed with cancer, and Ellie would often find herself getting stressed out and panicked. And now, all these years later, she still relied on it to soothe herself.

Cupping her hands under the spray, she brought them to her face, splashing the water against her eyes, cheeks, and forehead, and letting it drip down her neck until her sweater grew damp. She stared at her reflection in the mirror, face glistening and wet, and then she reached for a paper towel, patted herself dry, and smoothed her long blond hair back into its usual ponytail.

As she headed out of the bathroom and toward class, she

vowed to be nicer to Anne. After all, it was ridiculous and rude not to be. Ellie knew she was pretty, popular, and smart, so there was really no reason to feel so threatened by some new girl.

Except for maybe the way Chris had looked at her.

Sliding onto her usual front row seat, Ellie opened her backpack and retrieved her new notebook and pens. She secretly loved the first day of school, with all the newly sharpened pencils and clean notebooks full of freshly lined paper. *There's something so hopeful about the first day of anything,* she thought.

Then, looking up just as the bell rang, she saw Lola charging through the door. Then she glanced nervously at Mr. Campbell, who was already standing at his podium, ready to take roll.

"Welcome, Lola," he said. "So glad you could join us." He smiled. Mr. Campbell taught all the Honors English classes, so he, Lola, and Ellie had a history together.

"I had one foot in the door before the bell actually started ringing. So technically this is not a tardy," Lola said, smiling and catching her breath.

She slipped into the same seat she'd had for the last two years—the one in the second row, right behind Ellie. "Did I miss anything?" she whispered, poking Ellie in the shoulder.

Ellie turned and smiled, noticing her hair was back in its ponytail and her sweater was once again covering her tiny top. Lolita was gone for now. "Only the new girl," Ellie told her, turning and nodding toward Anne, who was sitting in the far corner.

"The blond one?" Lola asked, craning her neck to get a better look. "In the black sweater and jeans?"

"Yeah," Ellie said, rolling her eyes despite her recent pledge to be nice.

"She's really pretty. Have you talked to her?" Lola asked.

"A little." Ellie shrugged, suddenly wishing she hadn't mentioned her now that Lola was so curious.

"Is she nice?"

Ellie watched Lola smile and wave when Anne looked over at her. *Why the hell did she have to do that?* Ellie thought. *Why does she have to be so . . . welcoming?* They'd been a tight-knit group forever. The last thing they needed was some overdressed East Coast non-surfing snob to come along and mess things up. It was like the more Ellie found herself surfing alone, the more she worried she was losing her friends. And it wasn't like she expected them to love all the same things she loved. She respected their differences. But surfing used to be the one thing they all loved equally. And now it seemed like she was left holding the board while they all drifted off toward other, new interests.

Ellie had never feared change until the summer her mother died. Her mom had somehow managed to outlive her prognosis by six months, and even though Ellie knew she was dying, she somehow refused to believe it until it actually happened. She was just twelve years old and it felt like her own life had ended. And the only thing that had gotten her through it, the only thing that kept her from going completely mental, was her friendship with Lola and Jade, and the routine she slowly built for herself and managed to stick to, no matter what.

Every single day Ellie made herself surf, study, and achieve something. Whether it was winning a school election, running a quicker mile on the treadmill at the gym, or getting the highest grade on an exam, she was completely obsessed with winning, being perfect, and having complete control of her life. Having learned at an early age that the biggest and most important things were completely beyond her reach, she was now determined to conquer the small stuff.

Though she had one creative outlet for all that nervous ambition. One activity that she allowed herself to just merely enjoy

with no competition or harsh self-judgment. But it belonged only
to her, and no one else knew about it.

"Uh, *hello?* Earth to Ellie!"

Ellie shook her head and looked at Lola, realizing her friend
was still waiting for a response. "Oh, the new girl? She's okay, I
guess." She shrugged.

"Well, she's sure got great taste in shoes. Look at those boots!
I've seriously gotta find out where she scored them," Lola said,
smiling in the way that lit up rooms, made clouds disappear, and
guys fall to their knees. Lola was like the Julia Roberts of Laguna
Beach High. No one could be mad, angry, or depressed when she
smiled.

Ellie smiled back, then turned to face the front of the room. She
loved Lola for her constant optimism. But there was no way she
was going to look at Anne (or her stupid boots) any more than
she had to.

chapter nine

Anne was not having a very good first day. Having gone to the same private school all of her life, with pretty much the same group of people, she was not enjoying the novelty of being the new girl. Not one bit. And by the time lunch rolled around, the thought of eating anything out of the bag Christina had packed completely nauseated her. Her stomach felt tight with nerves and self-pity. And even though she'd promised herself she would wait until she got home to call Justin, the second the lunch bell rang she pulled out her cell phone and went looking for a quiet, shady spot where they could talk.

Sinking down onto a patch of grass, she waited while it rang one, two, three times.

"Hello?" he said, his voice sounding so clear that she immediately closed her eyes and imagined him sitting right next to her.

"Hey," she said softly, her throat going tight with emotion.

"How's it going?" he asked. "It's your first day, right?"

"Um, yeah. It's going okay," she said, not wanting to let on just exactly how far things were from okay. She didn't want him to worry about her. "It's lunchtime here, so I just thought I'd call and say hey." God, she sounded so forced. Why did she feel so uncomfortable talking to him now? They'd been together for a year and a half. They'd shared *everything* together, well—*almost* everything. Sometimes she wished they'd gone all the way on their very last night together. But right now she somehow felt relieved that they hadn't. Everything just felt so distant and weird.

"Listen, school just let out and I'm getting a ride home from Vanessa."

"Vanessa's there?" she asked, trying not to sound overly paranoid even though she had good reason. Vanessa was Justin's next-door neighbor and former on-and-off girlfriend from grade one through eight. On the surface, she and Vanessa always acted like they got along really well. But in reality, they both knew better. Vanessa wasn't over Justin, and Anne knew it. "What happened to your car?" she asked, trying to keep her voice even, less panicked.

"It's in the shop."

"For how long?"

"At least a few days. Hey, can I call you later? Vanessa's honking, so I gotta go before she leaves without me."

"Oh, I doubt she'll leave without you," Anne said, feeling like a pathetic, jealous wife.

"What?" he asked. "I'm losing you."

And then he was gone.

Well, he may not be losing me, she thought, flipping her phone closed and lying back on the grass. But she wondered if she was losing him.

By the time Jake picked her up from school Anne was feeling so depressed and so low that she walked right up to the silver Mercedes, plopped onto the passenger seat, and slammed the door so quick and hard she barely missed her own foot.

"So how'd it go?" he asked, waving at some people he knew as he pulled out of the parking lot.

"I-don't-want-to-talk-about-it," she said, slumping down in the seat and closing her eyes against the overbearing, totally relentless California sun. *Does every day always have to be so sunny and bright? Can't it ever be just a little damp, dark, and dreary for those of us with a happiness deficiency?*

She glanced over at Jake, practically daring him with her eyes to say something positive, because then she'd really let him have it. But he just shrugged and turned up the stereo.

When he pulled into the driveway, he turned to her. "Your dad's coming home."

"Really?" she said, sounding excited in spite of herself.

"Yeah, he called this morning, he'll be here on Thursday. Friday at the latest. But for sure by the weekend."

Anne just grabbed her books and got out of the car. So it was finally official. She'd been abandoned by *both* her parents now, and quite possibly her boyfriend, too. She was tempted to call Child Protective Services.

"Don't be so bummed," Jake said, following her inside. "Most kids would be stoked to have a house like this to themselves."

"Yeah, well it's not like I have any friends to party with," she said, throwing her bag on the kitchen counter and wishing she hadn't actually said that out loud. It made her sound so pathetic.

"Relax. It'll happen," he said, grabbing two bottles of water from the fridge and handing her one. "I can introduce you to lots of people."

Anne took a sip of water and looked at him. She knew he was just trying to be helpful and make her feel better, but it's not like she really wanted to hang with him. "Thanks," she said. "But I'll work it out."

He nodded and started to head back toward the door.

"So what are you doing now?" she called after him.

"I was just gonna grab my board and head out for a while. Why? Do you need something?"

"Actually," she said, looking down at her stupid outfit that hadn't helped her blend in anywhere except for maybe in the teacher's lounge. "I need to get a few things at the mall."

"You want me to take you to the mall?" he asked, looking completely bummed.

"No, I was wondering if you'd leave me the keys?" She smiled, realizing she hadn't done that in a while. "I can drive myself."

"Do you even know where it is?"

"Jake, *I'm a girl*. I'm sure I can find the mall," she told him, hoping his love of surf would override his work ethic.

He stood there for a moment, looking at her and weighing his options. Then his eyes wandered over to the huge windows and the ocean view. "I'll MapQuest the directions for you," he said, heading into the home office.

chapter ten

By Friday, Anne had talked to her parents on the phone for a combined total of six times. Her mom had called both Tuesday and Thursday mornings before school, with each conversation ending in a very ugly emotional argument. And her dad had phoned faithfully every evening, full of apologies, yet completely trusting in his little protégé, Jake, to look after her. But Anne rarely argued with her dad, even when he completely annoyed her, like now. Though his deadline was tonight, eight o'clock max. Okay, maybe eight thirty. But no later. She was done waiting for him.

She was also done with feeling like a victim. Because even though she hadn't made any real friends yet, she was determined to stop feeling so sorry for herself all the time and instead try to stay focused on the small victories. Like on Tuesday, when she wore some of the new clothes she'd purchased during her visit to South Coast Plaza, and how she'd blended in with all the students she was still too shy to talk to. And on Wednesday, when having helped herself to the car keys while Jake was out on the deck drinking a beer with friends, she'd cruised around in the silver Mercedes, top down, hair getting tangled in the wind, until she located a gym where she could work out and try to stay in shape on the off chance she ever found a place where she could start diving again. And on Thursday, when Chris had followed her out of AP History, loosely flung his arm around her shoulder, and tried to lead her to the lunch tables where he hung with his friends. But even though she was really tempted to join him and maybe meet some people she could actually talk to, she had a telephone appointment with Justin that she just couldn't break. She knew there was something going on with him, and she was determined to get to the bottom of it.

"I'm sorry, but I can't," she'd said, ducking out from under Chris's arm.

"What do you mean? Come on, everybody's really cool," he'd said, flashing that megawatt smile of his.

"I know, but I promised my boyfriend I'd call him," she'd told him, wondering if that was still the appropriate title for Justin.

"Oh, sorry." He looked really embarrassed. "I didn't know." He held his hands up in surrender, and backed away. "I guess I'll see ya later then," he had called, turning and jogging toward the lunch tables, leaving Anne standing there alone and wondering if she'd just made a major mistake.

In retrospect, it had been a mistake. Since after going to that pathetic patch of grass that had become her usual, lonely lunch-time hangout, she sat cross-legged in the sun and made her usual, desperate bid to communicate with Justin. She flipped open her cell, pushed the right buttons, and let it ring itself all the way into voice mail.

So then she called again.

And then one more time.

And then, finally deciding to call his house and speak to his mother, she was promptly informed that Justin was next door.

"Would you like me to run over and get him?" she'd asked.

"Um, no. That's okay," Anne had said, closing her phone and lying flat on the grass, eyes closed against the sun, refusing to cry.

Justin lived on the corner.

Which meant he only had *one* next-door neighbor.

Which meant he was at Vanessa's! Apparently he no longer cared about their scheduled telephone time!

Oh God. "Telephone time"—it even sounds pathetic! She rolled over onto her stomach, burying her face in the warm grass. What had they been thinking? Had she really believed they could make it work with all those miles between them? And when they promised they'd wait for each other, what exactly did that even mean? Because from what she knew about Vanessa, she doubted Justin would be waiting for anything.

She'd sat up, rubbed her eyes, and squinted at some guys throwing a Frisbee around the quad, some cheerleaders on a bench comparing manicures, and Chris telling a story, motioning wildly with his hands, while everyone around him laughed.

She lived here now. Not Connecticut. And her first big romance was over. Strangely, she didn't feel so bad about it.

chapter eleven

Lola was in her mom's bathroom, lounging in the awesome oversized Jacuzzi tub and enjoying the hot water, the bubbles, and the candles that were lit all around her as only a luxury-loving girl could. She lifted her leg high into the air, watching the bubbles gather, skidding into each other and slipping down to her knee. Then she stared at her feet, noting that her pedicure was definitely past its prime, but hoping she could pass it off for just one more night. She was determined to wear her new metallic stilettos on her date.

Her date. For her seventeen years, Lola had already been on many dates—far more than most girls her age. The very first one took place in sixth grade at the Ocean Ranch Cinemas when she had told her mom she was seeing *How the Grinch Stole Christmas* with Ellie and Jade, when what she really saw was *Almost Famous* with Parker Knowles, the cutest boy in her class. Lola had walked out of that theater wanting to be just like Penny Lane. Except for the drugs. And the getting traded to another band for a case of beer. Not to mention that unfortunate overdose. But still, everything else just seemed so glamorous, especially the furry-collared coat, the black sunglasses, and how all the guys in the movie fell in love with her.

Up until then, Parker Knowles had been one of her longest last-
ing, most serious romances. They'd been boyfriend and girlfriend
for the better part of three weeks.

But things were simpler back then. Going steady meant no
more than a handful of awkward phone calls, some sweaty hand-
holding, and a few embarrassing attempts at kissing. By the time
she and Parker had gotten it right, it was over. And so Lola
quickly moved on to a succession of junior-high crushes, one vir-
tually indistinguishable from the next.

Lola loved boys. She loved funny, straightforward, athletic,
smart boys. She didn't like the ones that acted overly cool, or
dressed overly hip, or tried too hard to get noticed. Though she
did like it when they fell to her feet. But pretty as she was, it was
her smile that always reeled them in. From the moment she
smiled, guys turned to putty, willing to do just about anything she
asked.

But as much as she loved boys in general, she had never loved
one in particular. Until this past summer, when everything
changed.

They'd met before. But this time was different. And the girl who
all her friends went to for advice (as though all that dating had
made her more worldly, when the truth was she was just as much
a virgin as they were) suddenly found herself completely clueless at
how to proceed. So she'd spent the entire time concentrating on
acting completely normal in front of her friends, even flirting with
a couple other guys just out of habit. But her eyes followed *him*
constantly. And if she wasn't mistaken, she was sure he'd been
watching her, too.

They'd met up again at the Ocean Ranch Golden Spoon, standing in line next to each other and both laughing when they ordered the exact same thing—a regular half pistachio–half vanilla
with yogurt chips (she'd ordered first, so if anyone was copying, it
was *him*). Then they'd carried their cups outside and sat at one of

the small round tables, talking until her plastic spoon scraped against the bottom of the cup, and there was nothing left.

The second time was not an accident. Although it was a secret. As had been every single date that followed. Until, slowly, Lola began to realize that the strange, sometimes painful feeling in the pit of her stomach, accompanied by her newfound obsession with hours and minutes and seconds (counting them until she'd get to see him again), was the exhilarating, thrilling, and somewhat scary feeling of being in love.

Too bad she couldn't confide in her friends. Or her parents. Or anyone else, for that matter. It meant way too much to her to just put it out there for other people to judge. And she knew the only way to protect it was to keep it close, and quiet, and secret.

She feared that her friends, knowing what a big flirt she'd always been, wouldn't take her seriously. Not to mention how they'd totally freak at her choice. And there was no doubt that Ellie would be the first (and worst) to judge. And so Lola, being a total people pleaser, had even flirted with that guy in the Jeep just to keep up the appearance of her "normal" self. But all the while she'd been thinking about someone else.

And she couldn't tell her parents because they, along with *Abuela,* would have a complete and total meltdown. Because for starters, he wasn't Mexican. Or Spanish. Or Puerto Rican. Or Panamanian or Argentinean or any other form of Hispanic that her parents would have grudgingly accepted after Mexican. And he wasn't interested in having the "right kind of job." He was an athlete, an artist, an innovator—a true renaissance man—but she knew her parents would not be impressed.

Right now Lola felt so insanely, blissfully happy that she just couldn't take any chances on having someone else wreck it.

"Lola?" her mother called, walking into the bathroom and leaning against the marble sink.

"Mom, I'm trying to take a bath here, jeez," she said, sinking way down so she was covered up to her neck in bubbles.

"We're leaving in an hour," her mother said, turning toward the mirror and checking her makeup.

"Okay." Lola picked up a bottle of body scrub and poured some into her palm. As far as she was concerned, the sooner they left, the better. She had lots of prepping to do for tonight, and it would all go a lot smoother if they weren't around to supervise.

"Will you be ready by then?" Her mother turned to face her.

"Ready for what?" she asked, getting a sick feeling in the pit of her stomach. "What are you talking about?" Lola had no idea what her parents had in store for her, but there was no way they would keep her from going on her date.

"Tonight's that movie screening, and your father is insisting that you go."

"What? No!" Lola said, her heart racing as she looked at her mother and pleaded. "Mom, I can't, okay? I have plans." *God, it's like they're determined to wreck my life!* She'd had a serious boyfriend for exactly three months now, and she was thinking about doing something very major to mark the occasion. It might be too soon, but she loved him so much it would probably be worth it. And she knew her dad didn't care if she went to the stupid premiere. This was her mom's doing. She was always trying to show off her pretty daughter and get her noticed by Hollywood. Even though Lola herself had no interest in any of it.

"This is very important to your father and me. You will come with us, and that's final," she said, turning to leave as though everything was settled.

"*No!* Mom, I'm serious!" Lola begged. "It's Friday night and I have plans!"

"Well, I'm very sorry you made plans, because you've known about this for over a week now."

Was that true? Had she known about it? Because she had absolutely no recollection of having been told. Was being in love giving her amnesia? "Mom, please, I'm *so* not joking. I'll do anything to make it up to you guys. Just please don't ask me to do this, *please*!"

"What on earth is so important?" her mother asked, crossing her arms coolly and surveying her wet, soapy, panicked daughter.

"I promised Ellie," she started. *Think, Lola, think!* "Um, you know how her mom died, like five years ago this month? Well, we always get together to kind of memorialize it." Okay, it wasn't a total lie, because they really did do that, and she was stopping there first. But still, using that for an excuse is definitely a guaranteed one-way ticket to Hell. Especially since what she was *really* planning to do was something her parents had always told her *would* send her to Hell.

"Fine." Her mother shook her head and sighed. "We'll take separate cars. You can drive mine. But you must come by as soon as you're finished. The screening is at eight. Don't be late," she said, giving her a stern look.

"Okay." Lola nodded, wondering what excuse she would use for when she didn't show. Ellie was too upset and she couldn't leave her? Ran out of gas? Wardrobe malfunction?

"And Lola?" her mother said, gripping the door handle.

"Yeah?"

"Don't even think about not showing up."

Lola watched until the door was completely closed. Then she took a deep breath and plunged under the bubbles, resting on the bottom of the tub for as long as she could.

chapter twelve

Anne was lounging on the couch, remote control in one hand, chip smothered in guacamole in the other, as she and Christina drank raspberry iced tea and watched Spanish-language *novelas* together. She'd been hanging out with Christina all day after school, and even though there was at least a twenty-year age gap, and definitely somewhat of a language barrier, she had to admit it beat hanging out by herself. Or, even worse, with Jake, who was always trying to get her into the ocean and onto a board.

But Anne refused to surf. And she refused to hang with people who surfed. And just for the record, she was also absolutely *done* with celebrating the "small victories." That sunny side up frame of mind had lasted an hour at best. And now she was right back to feeling sorry for herself.

It's the inventory that was so pathetic:

Friends—0.

Boyfriends—0.

Pool—0.

Diving board—0.

Dad (still missing in action)—0.

Anything remotely resembling her former life as she knew it—0.

She rolled her eyes at her sorry existence, then grabbed another chip and pulled it through the bowl of guacamole—twice. Then, holding it up in front of her, she looked over at Christina and smiled before shoving the entire thing into her mouth.

But Christina didn't smile back. Her eyes were busy watching the action on the flat screen TV. So Anne picked up another chip, repeating the same routine and wondering if maybe she should slow down just a bit since for the past hour or so her jeans had begun to feel a little, well, *confining*.

And, to be honest, hanging with Christina wasn't all it was cracked up to be. Anne had originally hoped that by asking her to stay late, they could hang out, have some fun, maybe get to know each other a little better. Thinking that in no time they'd be giggling and sharing inside jokes—*in Spanish, even*.

But now, as she undid her top button and grabbed another chip, it was becoming very clear just how misguided her plan had been. Not to mention the sad truth that Christina had probably only stayed because she thought she *had* to, and not because she *wanted* to.

chapter thirteen

The third week of September was always hard for Ellie. Not only did the responsibilities of school and home always threaten to overwhelm her, but it also marked the week her mom had died. September eighteenth, to be exact. And even though five years had passed, and it was slowly starting to get easier, whenever that day approached she always felt like a big dimmer switch had been put on her life. Everything just seemed so much darker.

With her brother always so busy and rarely around, and her father's refusal to ever mention it, she sometimes felt like she was the only one who remembered her, the only one who missed her, and the only one who hadn't gotten on with her life.

Slipping into a pair of clean khaki shorts, a white ribbed tank top, and some flip-flops, she left her long hair loose and wavy like her mom had always liked it. Then she went down the stairs and onto the beach, looking for her friends, wondering if they'd show, or if they'd even remember since it's not like it was something they organized.

It had started sort of organically, over the past few years, with the three of them just always congregating on the beach in the early-evening hours after school, and they'd laugh and talk and reminisce about all the good times. And there were never any candles, never any music, and rarely any crying. It was much more about celebrating her life than remembering her death.

Ellie sat on the old, scarred wood bench, enjoying the warmth of the sun-baked seat against the back of her legs. Some kids were out there surfing, and she felt a pang of guilt, knowing she should be out there, too. Especially if she didn't want to totally humiliate herself at the Surf Fest. But this day wasn't about surfing. It was one of the few days when she gave herself a break.

"Hey, Ellie!" Ellie looked up to see Jade smiling and waving, with her brown curls bouncing as she jogged toward her.

Ellie waved back, feeling relieved that she wouldn't have to go it alone this year. She knew that someday she would, but she was glad it wasn't now. Right now, she just wasn't ready.

chapter fourteen

Lola stood in front of the mirror, dripping water all over the mosaic-tiled floor, wondering how her life had gotten so complicated. True, she may have been just the tiniest bit responsible for keeping secrets from those she loved, but was it really such a bad thing to want to make everyone around you happy?

Her parents had already taken off. So that left only *Abuela,* who, hating all things Hollywood (despite her son's huge success as an entertainment lawyer), was firmly planted in the den watching TV in one of her ubiquitous housedresses.

Lola knew it would be easy enough to sneak past her and avoid her usual ploy of dressing in layers (sexy covered by conservative), but she knew it'd look strange and elicit all kinds of questions if she showed up on the beach to hang with Ellie and Jade in a pair of silver stilettos. *God, I never get a break!* And tonight would require no less than *three* costume changes—one for Ellie, one for her date, and one for her parents and that stupid movie screening.

She pulled her hair back into a sleek, low ponytail and put on the diamond studs she got for her sixteenth birthday, dropping her favorite silver hoops into the little pocket in her purse for later. Then she hurriedly stepped into a white terry-cloth sundress and ran out the door and down the street. She had almost made it to the top of the beach stairs when her cell rang.

"Hello?" she answered hastily. She had no time to talk, no time to waste.

"Hey," he said. It was him!

"Oh," she giggled. "I didn't look at the display—I didn't realize it was you."

"You sound like you're in a hurry."

"Well, kind of. I mean, I have to meet Ellie right now, and then my parents are insisting that I go to this movie screening thing with them." She rolled her eyes instinctively.

"I thought we were having dinner?"

"We are! I can fit it all in, trust me. I just have to juggle a few things around, that's all."

"Lola," he started.

"Trust me. I can make it work. I just might not be able to see you 'til a little later than we planned, that's all."

"I made reservations for eight," he said, his voice sounding tight.

"Oh. Well, can you change them? Because that's when I'm supposed to be in L.A."

"Change them to what? Right now for the early-bird special?" He sounded angry.

"Listen, you don't have to feed me. I can grab some popcorn at the movie, and then we can still see each other later." She felt like she was begging, just like she had earlier with her mother. "I can't wait to see you," she whispered.

"Lola," he sighed. "I've been thinking . . ."

Oh God, don't say that. Don't think! She grabbed the handrail.

"Maybe this isn't such a great idea."

She sunk down onto the top step and rested her forehead against her knees.

"It's like, maybe this just isn't good timing for us. You're still in high school, still living with your parents . . ."

"You still live at home!" she said, feeling kind of angry. *It's not like he didn't know all that. He'd always known all that.*

"Yeah, but it's different for me."

"What are you trying to say?" she asked, but only because she had to. Not because she wanted to hear the answer.

"I just think it's better if we take it easy for a while. Let things cool down a bit . . ."

She just sat there, holding the phone but not daring to speak into it. *Breathe,* she thought. *All that's required of you is to breathe.*

"Lola?" His voice sounded small, far away.

"I have to go," she whispered, closing her phone, fixing her ponytail, and running down the rest of the stairs to meet Ellie and Jade.

chapter fifteen

Anne was just contemplating changing into something with an elastic waist and opening another bag of chips when she heard a key turning in the lock.

"Is anyone home?" her dad called, dropping his bag with an audible thump and heading down the hall.

Giving Christina a guilty look, she wiped the crumbs from her face, sucked in her belly, and buttoned her jeans again. "Um, we're in here," she yelled, hurriedly grabbing a napkin to dab at a guacamole stain on her sloppy gray T-shirt. "In the den."

When she looked up and saw him standing in the doorway, she realized how much she'd missed him. "Hey, Dad," she said, smiling and getting up to hug him. Maybe it was just her imagination, but he seemed a little surprised to find her watching Telemundo with Christina.

"How've you been?" he asked, looking from one to the other.

"*Sí*, fine," Christina said, smiling and grabbing another chip.

"Um, we were just hanging out," Anne said, seeing it from his point of view and realizing it probably did look a little strange. "Christina's been helping me with my Spanish. Well, kind of." She shrugged.

"That's very nice," he said, nodding at Christina. "That's very—*bueno*."

"Looks like you could use a little help with yours, too," Anne said, laughing.

"So do you have any plans tonight?" he asked his daughter.

"Um, this is pretty much it." She shrugged sheepishly. "My first week at school hasn't been the social whirl you might think," she admitted.

"Feel like hanging out with your old man?"

"Yeah, sure," she said, no longer feeling angry with him for being gone all week. She just wanted to spend some time with him again. "But if you were thinking about dinner, I'm really not hungry." She ran a finger between the waist of her jeans and her skin, trying to loosen them up a little, but her finger got stuck.

"That's okay; I can grab something there. Why don't you hop in the shower and get changed while I give Christina a ride home so she can spend some time with her family," he said, smiling and nodding at Christina, so she'd at least know he was talking to her even if she didn't know what he was saying.

Christina has a family? Anne thought. *Oh God, she must hate me for keeping her here!*

"And when I get back, I'll take you to a Hollywood screening. There'll be paparazzi, so wear something nice," he said, eyeing the avocado stain on her top.

Anne looked at her dad, the truth slowly sinking in. This wasn't about spending quality time with his daughter. Oh no. This was about work. It was always about work. And now, with her mom gone, apparently she would be the one he would drag to all of his functions. Oh well, it beat watching soap operas she didn't understand, and carbo-loading. "How long have I got?" she asked.

"Is forty-five minutes enough?"

"You're pushing it, but I'll be ready," she said, waving good-bye to Christina and heading into her room.

chapter sixteen

"Have you talked to Lola?" Ellie asked, scanning the beach once again, but still not seeing her.

"No, but she'll make it, don't worry." Jade smiled and sat down next to her friend. "I can't believe it's been five years already," she said, eyeing Ellie carefully.

"I know; it went so fast. But then, in a way, it didn't, you know?" Ellie said.

Jade nodded. "So, how's your dad?" she asked. Jade always found Ellie's dad to be more than a little intimidating. It's not that he was mean or anything; it's just that ever since he'd lost his wife he'd become hardened, almost aggressive, like he was some underdog fighting to get to the top, when the truth was, he was already at the top. And Jade couldn't imagine what further career goals an oncologist and chief of staff at Hoag Hospital could possibly have. But then again, maybe that's what extreme tragedy did to people—made them coarser, less trusting, more driven.

Ellie's dad was a cancer specialist who couldn't save his own wife. Who hadn't even recognized the symptoms (even if they were practically invisible) until it was far too late. And being completely unable to forgive himself, it was like he'd descended into these awful feelings of extreme self-doubt and failure. And having always been kind of a control freak in the past, he now focused all of his attention on the one thing he thought was still in his control—Ellie.

Jade shook her head and sighed. She'd always been interested in what made people tick. But she felt lucky that in this particular case she only had to guess at the truth and not actually live it, like poor Ellie.

"He's okay." Ellie shrugged. "Still on my case all the time, but he means well. And it really does help me stay focused and on track."

Jade looked at her friend. She was always so ready to defend her dad, but that's probably because he was all she had left. "But on track for *what* exactly?" she asked carefully. She never fully understood her friend's unwavering determination. It didn't seem to make her any happier, and it always seemed to come at the expense of everything else.

"*College*. I *have* to go to a good school. I don't want to be hanging around here forever. And you know how much I've been wanting a surf sponsorship."

Ellie seemed on edge, but Jade was determined to finally have the conversation she'd been mulling over for a while now. So she proceeded cautiously. "I don't know, El. It's like, well, remember when we first started surfing? How your mom taught us because your brother and his friends were making fun of us?"

They both smiled at the memory. Ellie's brother, Dean, was two years older, gorgeous, cool, and a great surfer, so of course all three girls had idolized him. But he and his friends wanted nothing to do with them. Surfing was a "boy's" sport, and they always got a good laugh watching the girls struggling to stay on their boards. One day Ellie's mom saw what was going on and packed them up, took them over to another beach, and nearly every day for the next several weeks patiently taught the girls to surf until they were good enough, and confident enough, to hold their own. By the time they returned to Laguna Cove, the boys were no longer laughing.

"Well," Jade continued, "It seemed like you were different back then. Like you just loved being in the water, and at school it was like you just liked learning new stuff."

"What are you trying to say, Jade?" Ellie eyed her warily.

"Well, what I mean is, sometimes I worry that you're not really *loving* this stuff anymore. And if you're not really loving something, then like, what's the point?" She looked at her friend carefully, but Ellie was staring off into the horizon, and Jade wondered if she had just stopped listening.

They sat quietly for a while; then Ellie looked at Jade and said, "I know you worry about me. But I worry about you, too. Only for the exact opposite reason." She smiled.

Jade shrugged, then looked across the beach and said, "Hey, there's Lola."

They both looked over to see Lola smiling and waving, holding her flip-flops in one hand, while her bare feet carved into the sand as she made her way across the beach.

"Hey, you guys," she said, leaning in to hug first Ellie, then Jade.

"Are you okay?" Jade asked.

"Yeah, why?" Lola asked.

"I don't know. Your mascara's a little smudged, and all these years I've known you I've never seen your makeup anything less than perfect."

"Jeez. Cut me some slack, will ya?" Lola said, sitting on the bench across from her friends. "So did I miss anything?"

"We were just talking about when Ellie's mom taught us to surf," Jade said, eyeing Lola, still not convinced everything was so great. That amazing smile she always had seemed a little muted now.

"That's one of my best memories of her. Well, that and those orange chocolate-chip oatmeal cookies she used to make," Lola said.

"And don't forget how she crocheted those matching sky blue bikinis for all of us," Jade added.

"Oh God. We thought we were so hot in those," Ellie laughed.

"Yeah, until they came off in the water!" Lola laughed.

"Right in front of those boys!" Jade said. "Too bad for them we were only ten, so there wasn't much to see!"

"Speak for yourself," Lola said. "I was stunning at ten!"

"Sorry, Lola, we still had baby fat. Ellie was the stunning one." Jade smiled, looking at Ellie, who had turned bright red. She'd never been good at receiving compliments.

"So what are you guys doing later?" Ellie asked.

"I'm supposed to go to this stupid movie premiere with my parents," Lola said, rolling her eyes.

"Must be rough," Jade and Ellie said simultaneously.

"Yeah, yeah. I don't mean to sound like a brat. I kind of had other plans, but I guess they just got canceled," Lola said, suddenly looking away from her friends and toward the waves crashing in front of them.

"So, postpone," Ellie said. "You've always managed to sneak out of those in the past. So what's the big deal now?"

"Well, apparently he wasn't up for a reschedule." Lola pressed her lips together and stood up suddenly.

"Are you leaving?" Jade asked, eyeing her friend with concern.

Lola nodded.

"Well, in case you do manage to escape. There's a party tonight at Aliso Beach. You should stop by. Ellie and I will be there."

"I will?" Ellie asked, looking at Jade. It was the first she'd heard of it.

"*Yes*, you are going with me. In fact, you're driving. In fact, you're the designated driver. Anyway, try to make it, Lolita; it's gonna be fun."

Lola just looked at them and shrugged. Then she turned and made her way back up the beach.

chapter seventeen

Anne sat next to her dad in the crowded, darkened theater, watching the other audience members more than the action on screen. *Or the lack of action,* she thought. The movie was a total bore. But in the audience there were a few people she recognized from *People* magazine covers and award shows. Like, just two rows up, wasn't that Renee Richards? And who was that scruffy guy she was making out with? Anne figured he must be really important, because as her father once explained to her, the more power you had in Hollywood, the more you could dress down.

She glanced quickly at her dad, mindlessly eating popcorn and shaking his head and smirking at the screen. *Well, at least we're in agreement about the movie sucking!*

She leaned toward him and whispered, "I'll be right back; I'm gonna find the bathroom."

He looked at her briefly and nodded, then quickly focused his attention back on the screen.

She made her way up the dark aisle, at one point tripping on some supermodel's shoe. The model gave her a nasty look. *Oh yeah, like it's my fault your legs are six feet long and can't fit in a normal-sized space,* she thought, rolling her eyes right back at her.

Exiting the theater, she squinted against the brightness of the movie ads, popcorn machines, and the oversized chandelier that would surely squash anybody unlucky enough to be standing underneath during an earthquake. Not that she'd ever been in an earthquake, but now that she was living in California, she thought about them a lot.

Finding the restroom, she pushed inside and after inspecting her makeup in the mirror and washing her hands, she plopped down onto a little velvet settee and closed her eyes.

She'd been sitting like that for five, ten minutes max, when someone rushed by so fast Anne barely got a look at her. Then she heard the stall door slam and lock. Then there was some very loud crying.

Anne just sat there, wondering if she should offer to help. On the one hand, it was clearly none of her business. There was no way she knew the girl, since she didn't know anyone here except for her dad. But on the other hand, the girl sounded so seriously distressed that it made it hard to just sit there and do nothing. *But what if she just wants to be left alone?*

Okay, Anne decided, *I'll offer to help.* If she wasn't interested, Anne would just go back into the theater and leave her in peace.

Just as she was getting up to investigate, the door slammed open and this tiny girl with long, dark hair, dressed in cute jeans, a white blouse, a black shrunken blazer, and awesome silver stilettos looked at her and said, "Hey, I know you."

"You do?" Anne asked, wondering how the girl could possibly know her.

"You go to Laguna High, right? You're that new girl," she said, rubbing a hand across her eyes and smearing her makeup even more.

"Yeah, I'm Anne," she said, thinking that now that the girl was right in front of her, she did look familiar.

"I'm Lola." She plopped herself down on the chair across from Anne and smiled ruefully.

"Are you okay?" Anne asked carefully, wondering if she was supposed to say anything or just pretend like a face full of smeared makeup was all the rage in the OC.

"Actually no, I'm not. I'm dying, I'm devastated, and I've been dumped," she said, shaking her head and digging through her purse. "And now I can't even find a tissue." Her eyes welled up with tears again.

"Hang on. Here," Anne said, handing her a crumpled one she'd found at the bottom of her bag. "It's clean, too, I swear." She watched Lola blow her nose over and over and over again, wondering how one little tissue could actually withstand all that.

"Thanks," she said, wadding it up and tossing it into the trash. Then she curled her legs up under her. "Sorry about all this. My parents insisted I come to this stupid thing, and because of it I got dumped. And believe me, it's not the first time they've interfered." She shook her head. "It's just so hard when they expect so much from me. I mean, they never would have approved of him, and that's why it all had to be a big secret. But I think he got tired of sneaking around." She stopped and looked at Anne. "And you want to know the worst part?"

Anne just nodded, not entirely sure that she did. She wasn't used to people just spilling their guts like this. But then she remembered how her dad had once told her that in movie speak this was called a California Conversation. Apparently this kind of soul dumping was routine for those who lived here.

"I was actually considering doing something *really* major with him, you know? God, I'm such an idiot," she said, covering her face with her hands and starting to cry again.

"Don't say that. You should be glad that you didn't, because now you don't have anything big to regret, right?" Anne said softly.

Lola looked up, nodding slowly.

"Just be glad you found out now." Anne smiled.

"God, I can't believe I just told you all that when my best friends don't even know." Lola looked suddenly panicked. "Oh God, *please* don't mention this to Ellie and Jade. They'll freak."

"Don't worry," Anne assured her. "Jade's in my art class, but we don't sit by each other. And Ellie, well, I don't think she likes me enough to ever have a conversation with me."

Lola looked at Anne and shrugged. "Ellie's cool. Really. She's just a little leery of newcomers, that's all."

Anne didn't say anything. She wasn't sure she believed that.

"Did you have a boyfriend in—where'd you move from?"

"Connecticut, and yeah, I did. His name was Justin and he just dumped me for his old girlfriend. Didn't take him long to move on, did it?" Anne said, relieved that she could finally say it out loud without choking up. Even though it did feel kind of weird to talk about him in the past tense.

"Hey." Lola looked at her and smiled in a way that lit up her whole face despite the mascara trails running down her cheeks. "This movie *blows*. What do you say we bail? I heard there's this party tonight at Aliso Beach. It's just gonna be a bunch of people from school, but it's gotta be better than this."

"But what am I gonna tell my dad?" Anne asked, feeling torn between wanting to hang with Lola and leaving her dad, who she'd barely spent any time with. *But*, was that her fault, or his?

"Tell him you don't feel well and I'm taking you home. And I'll tell my parents the same thing. Come on; it'll be fun," she said, opening her compact and surveying the damage.

"Okay. It's not like he'll miss me, anyway. He's too busy staring at the screen and inhaling popcorn. He probably won't even notice I'm gone," Anne said, hoping that wasn't exactly true.

"My mom's not even watching the movie. She's too busy sitting next to Renee Richards, hoping someone will take a picture of the two of them." She rolled her eyes.

"Did you see that guy she's making out with?" Anne asked.

"You don't know the half of it. She's my dad's client. Come on," Lola said, standing up and grabbing her purse. "I'll fill you in on the drive to Orange County."

chapter eighteen

By the time Ellie and Jade were dressed and ready to leave, they'd worked up some major excitement about the party. Never mind that it would just be the same old people talking about the same old stuff. There was something about spending the afternoon with Jade and remembering all the good times with her mom that made Ellie feel lighter, more positive, and less willing to be so damn uptight.

They were in her Mini Cooper, just about to pull out of the driveway, when Ellie's father drove up. "Hey, Mr. Stone," Jade said, smiling and waving.

Barely acknowledging her with a brisk nod, he looked at Ellie and said, "Did you finish your homework?"

"Yes," Ellie said, still backing up slowly. She was determined to get out of there before he completely killed her buzz.

"Okay, but don't stay out too late. You need to be up early tomorrow. I've booked you a coach. She'll be here by eleven."

"A coach?" Ellie slammed on her brake. "Dad, I don't need a coach," she said.

"Of course you need her! And you should try to get in a few sessions before she shows."

"But Dad," she pleaded.

"No buts, it's already booked. Have a nice night," he said, climbing out of his convertible BMW and heading toward the front door.

Ellie focused on breathing, slow and deep, as she watched him open the door. *So much for being in a good mood,* she thought, backing out of the driveway and pulling onto the street.

chapter nineteen

"So aren't we a little overdressed for a beach party?" Anne asked, glancing at Lola's stilettos, then down at her own silk skirt.

"Probably." Lola shrugged. "But who cares. We'll just tell everyone we were at a big, glamorous Hollywood movie premiere. They'll be *sooo* jealous!" she laughed.

"Yeah, as long as we don't mention how bad it sucked!" Anne said, looking at Lola and smiling. She was finally having some fun, and it was all thanks to her. It was incredible how Lola had gone from choking, sobbing tears to looking completely glamorous. Anne wished she could be more like that. And after listening to Lola's nonstop chatter on the long drive down, apparently there was a lot she could learn from her. "So like, who's gonna be there? I mean, not that I really *know* anyone, but I do have most of the big names memorized." It was funny how everyone always knew the names of all the alphas, even when they didn't hang with them.

"All the usual suspects will be present and accounted for. You know, basically everyone from the lunch table." Lola smiled.

"Please, you don't even want to know where I've been eating

lunch," Anne said, looking out the window, and wondering why she had just confided that—it was kind of embarrassing.

"Well, my friend, that's all in the past. Now you will officially meet everyone and they will love you. I promise," Lola said, parking the car and rechecking her lip gloss in the rearview mirror. "And after they get to know you and see how great you are, I guarantee they will no longer call you the East Coast Ice Queen."

"*What?*" Anne said, getting out of the car and staring at her.

"Oh, maybe I shouldn't have told you that," Lola said, face full of regret. "Listen, *please* don't be upset. They only said that because you're so pretty but you kind of stick to yourself. You don't talk much." She shrugged.

"I get shy sometimes," Anne said, sounding really defensive and wondering if she still wanted to go to this party now that she knew what people were saying about her.

"Oh, come on." Lola looped her arm through Anne's. "What could be more fun than proving everyone wrong?"

They walked down the beach, toward the glowing bonfire, and of course, as luck would have it, the very first person Anne saw was the one who hated her the most, Ellie. She was sitting next to Jade and Chris and some guy named Duncan, and Lola was heading straight for them. Anne had the immediate urge to run in the opposite direction. She wasn't sure she was up for Ellie's dirty looks and cutting little comments. Ellie was probably the one who came up with the Ice Queen thing. But Lola was cool, and everyone else seemed okay, so if Ellie was determined to be a bitch, well, that was her problem.

"Hey, guys!" Lola said. "You remember Anne?"

Anne noticed Chris and Jade wave, but of course Ellie only narrowed her eyes and stared.

"We were just talking about surfing," Ellie said, completely ignoring Anne.

"But of course, what else is there?" Lola laughed, settling down onto the blanket and motioning for Anne to sit next to her.

"My dad got me a coach because the Surf Fest is next month, and he thinks I'm gonna choke like last year. It's so ridiculous." She shook her head. "I mean, what am I supposed to learn from a coach? I'm either gonna surf well or I'm not. And I just don't get how some trainer's gonna change that."

"I had a coach for my diving," Anne blurted out, before she could stop herself.

Ellie shook her head and rolled her eyes. "I really don't think that's the same thing," she said quickly. Then, turning back to everyone else, "*Anyway,* it just feels so—artificial. But apparently, Chris is on my dad's side." She smiled and poked him in the ribs, a little harder than she intended. She was completely hopeless at flirting, especially with a guy she really liked.

"Everything's different now," he said. "There's major big money in all the sponsorships, endorsements, and contests. A coach will just give you an edge, and maybe some techniques to deal with stress." He smiled.

"Who, me? Stress?" Ellie laughed. "Look, all I want is a sticker on my board. That's it, I swear."

"And a trophy, prize money, free clothes four times a year, and, oh yeah, your face on the cover of *SG* magazine." Lola laughed.

"You came really close last year," Jade reminded her.

"Yeah, until I choked." Ellie shook her head at the memory.

"Hence, the coach!" Chris said, laughing and throwing his arms in the air to make his point. Then, looking at Anne, he said, "So what's it gonna take to get you in the water?"

"Me?" Anne asked, surprised at being suddenly included.

"Yeah, you. I mean diving's great and all, but there's no dive team at school, so you might want to try it. Besides, you can't be a cliff dweller and not surf; it just ain't right. Right, Ellie?"

But Ellie didn't answer. And something about her absolute determination to ignore her, acting like she wasn't even worth talking to, made Anne so angry she went into full-blown flirt mode, just to mess with her. "Doesn't ice melt when it hits the water?" she asked, briefly touching Chris on the knee and smiling.

"What?" He looked at her carefully, while everyone else looked down at the ground, including Ellie.

"I told her. She knows *everything*," Lola said, looking at Anne and winking.

"We were just fooling around," Chris said quickly. "We didn't really mean it." He looked embarrassed and guilty.

"Hmmm." Anne looked at him. "I wonder how you could make it up to me?" She tossed her long blond hair over her shoulder and smiled.

"I'll teach you to surf," he offered.

"*You'll* teach me?" She gave him a skeptical look.

"Yeah, why not? I'm an okay surfer, wouldn't you agree?"

Lola and Duncan readily agreed, Ellie just glared, and Jade looked upset.

"I have to think about it," Anne said, feeling confused by the look on Jade's face and wondering if maybe she liked Chris too. She'd only been flirting with him to bug Ellie, but if all the girls were secretly fighting over him, then she would definitely back off. No matter how cute he was, it certainly wasn't worth upsetting everyone.

"Meet me on the beach tomorrow at noon," he said. "I won't take no for an answer. And remember, I know where you live."

Chris was looking at her and smiling, but Anne just sat there, not really sure what to do. It was her fault all the girls had gone all tense and quiet, and even though she was feeling too uncomfortable to look at her, she could feel Ellie's eyes burning right into her.

"So, who wants a beer?" Duncan asked, getting up and dusting the sand off his jeans.

Chris, Lola, Jade, and Anne all took a pass. But Ellie surprised everyone by jumping up, shaking her long shiny hair from its tight ponytail, and saying, "I'll have one."

"*You're* having a beer?" Jade and Lola said in unison, staring at their friend in disbelief.

Ellie looked annoyed. "Jeez, you guys, it's not like I've never had a drink before," she said, rolling her eyes and running to catch up with Duncan.

chapter twenty

By the time Ellie and Duncan were on their third beers the party was pretty much over. "So what do you want to do now?" he asked, leaning in 'til they were almost touching.

Ellie looked at him, his face so close to hers. And even though it was a really cute face, it definitely wasn't the right face. *It isn't Chris's face,* Ellie thought, glancing over at Chris, who was *still* flirting with Anne, as he had been all night, leaving Ellie with no choice but to flirt with someone else. But now, after all the joking, laughing, and hair tossing *(why does flirting come so easy when you aren't really all that into the person?),* she looked at Duncan, his brown eyes staring into hers, and she felt guilty, knowing she'd been leading him on and that he was way more into it than she was.

But as he looked in her eyes and leaned in even closer she suddenly thought, *Oh, what the hell? I mean, how bad could it really be?* He was cute, popular, smart, a decent surfer, and she'd known that he liked her since freshman year. She could trust him. And she knew she could trust herself not to like him too much.

The first thing she thought as his lips touched hers was, *I hope Chris is watching.*

The second thing was, *Hmmm—this isn't so bad . . .*

"Uh, you guys. Yoo-hoo! Sorry, I can see that you're very busy and all, but I just wanted to tell you I'm getting a ride home with Lola. Just so you don't worry when you come up for air. *If you come up for air,*" Jade said, obviously shocked by the sight of Ellie and Duncan making out.

Ellie pulled away and wiped her mouth with the back of her hand. Her face felt warm and raw from all the kissing, and her head felt weird from all the beer. "What?" She squinted at Jade.

"I'm taking off. So, um, good night," Jade said, giving an awkward little wave.

"Do you need a ride?" Ellie asked.

"Hmm," Jade said, looking them over. "Tell you what. Why don't you give *me* the keys, and I'll give *you guys* a ride. What do you say?"

"Don't be ridiculous. I'm perfectly capable of driving," Ellie said, rolling her eyes and attempting to stand, but her legs were not cooperating and she ended up right back on the sand, falling smack onto Duncan.

Jade stood there watching them, all tangled up together and laughing like it was *so hysterical.* "Okay, hand 'em over," she said, sounding like a chaperone while she reached for Ellie's keys.

chapter twenty-one

Anne woke to the sounds and smells of breakfast. A real breakfast. Like the kind her dad always used to make on the weekends, after a movie had wrapped and he had a little free time between projects.

She slipped into her terry-cloth robe and matching slippers and padded down the long tiled hallway to the kitchen. "Hey," she said, rubbing her eyes and reaching into the cupboard for a coffee mug.

"Hey, yourself," he said, turning briefly from the stove and smiling. "Feeling better?" he asked, raising one eyebrow.

"Okay, I confess. I wasn't really sick," she said, adding half-and-half to her coffee until it was light tan in color. "I met up with a friend from school and she invited me to a beach party. Are you mad?" She looked at him cautiously.

"No." He shook his head, and reached for two plates. "But you could have told me that." He came over to the table where she was sitting and handed her a plate full of eggs, toast, fruit, bacon—the works.

"I know. I didn't want to lie, but I also didn't want to make you feel bad since we haven't spent much time together," she said, inwardly thinking, *Not like that's my fault!*

"Well, you can make it up to me today. I thought we could go downtown, stroll around the galleries, have lunch, just relax," he said, taking a bite of his whole-grain toast.

Anne just looked at him. She wasn't exactly sure how to tell him that she wouldn't actually be able to "make it up" to him. "Um, well, I kind of made plans," she said, taking a sip of her coffee. "A friend has offered to teach me to surf. I'm supposed to meet him on the beach at noon."

"Don't worry about it," her dad said. "Go and have fun with your friends. In fact, it's funny you mentioned it, because I was thinking about getting back on a board myself."

"*You?*" Anne wished she hadn't sounded so incredulous, but the thought of her dad surfing was insane. He was *old*. He could get *hurt*! There was no way he could be serious. "What exactly do you mean, 'back on a board'?"

"Don't look so shocked. I used to surf," he said, taking a sip of his coffee.

"Uh, *when*? I mean, I've never seen any evidence of this." She shook her head and speared a piece of cantaloupe.

"Admittedly, it's been a few years, but I think I've still got it in me." He nodded. "I had a longboard. And I was pretty good, I'll have you know."

"Whatever, Dad," Anne said, finishing up her eggs. "Just please let me have the waves to myself today. No need for both of us to be humiliated."

At exactly six minutes past noon (she didn't want to look overly anxious), Anne headed down the stairs and onto the beach, looking for Chris. But not seeing him anywhere, she casually dropped her towel onto the sand, acting as though she wasn't at all concerned that she might very well possibly be getting stood up. *He did say noon, right?*

"Hey." She looked over to see Chris coming out of the water. His hair was slicked back, his board was under his arm, and even though she was trying not to stare, his body was cut, tanned, and totally amazing. "Glad to see we're still on. It's a good day to learn; the swells are kind of small," he said, smiling.

"I didn't really know what to bring," she said nervously, trying not to gawk at his six-pack abs. "So I just brought some sunscreen and a towel."

"No worries," he said. "I've got everything you need."

And when he smiled, she thought it might very well be true.

chapter twenty-two

Ellie's coaching lesson was not going well and it probably had a little something to do with the deep pool of regret she was currently wading in. Not to mention the hangover that had her not only fatigued and nauseous, but seriously longing to climb back into bed, pull the covers over her head, and forget about surfing, Surf Fest, and just about everything else.

It was Duncan, not her dad, who'd woken her this morning. And just hearing his voice had brought it all back. Her father was already at the hospital and her brother apparently didn't answer the phone anymore, so finally on the fifth ring she reached over and croaked, "Hello?"

"Ellie, did I wake you?" he'd said.

"Um yeah. Kind of. What time is it?" she'd asked.

"Ten thirty."

"Oh my God," she'd said, throwing off the sheets and jumping out of bed way too fast for her compromised condition. "Um, I gotta go. Can we talk later?" She fell back onto the mattress, gripped the edge, and closed her eyes against the banging in her head.

"Sure. I'll call you later," he'd said, sounding disappointed.

Oh, God. If that upset him, just wait 'til I tell him the truth, that

I made a huge mistake and should never have kissed him, she'd thought, feeling bad about the prospect but glad that she could put it off for a few more hours.

And now, out there in the ocean, all she wanted to do was float on her board, with the sun beating against her skin like a warm blanket while the gentle waves rocked her to sleep. She could think of nothing better.

"Maybe we should cut this short today," her coach, Lina, said.

"I'm sorry." Ellie slowly lifted her head and squinted at her. "I had kind of a rough night. And to be honest, I wasn't really into this to begin with. This was all pretty much my dad's idea." She rolled her eyes.

"Not a problem." Lina shrugged. "Either way, I'm still getting paid. But if you ever decide to get serious, give me a call," she said, heading for shore.

"Hey! Excuse me!" Ellie yelled after her. "But for your information, I *am* serious!" She sat up on her board and glared at the back of Lina's head, but all the while she wondered if it was true.

chapter twenty-three

Lola was almost out the door when she heard her mother call, "Lola? Can you come here for a minute?"

Oh God, I was so close, she thought, dutifully turning around and heading back into the kitchen to see what she could possibly want now.

"Oh, there you are," her mother said, leaning against the kitchen counter and sipping something out of a blue ceramic mug that Lola assumed contained her usual herbal tea concoction. "Did your friend get home okay last night?"

"What?" Lola squinted at her mom. "Oh, yeah," she said, suddenly remembering how she'd lied about Anne being sick. "Thanks for understanding," she added.

Her mother nodded. "I'm sorry you had to leave so early. There was someone there I wanted you to meet. So I gave him your number."

"What?" Lola dropped her beach bag onto the floor and stared at her. *She can't be serious. Please, dear God, don't let her be serious!*

"His name is Diego. He is the son of one of your father's associates. He's just a year ahead of you and I really think you two will hit it off." She smiled excitedly.

"But," Lola began, trying to think of a really good reason for why this could *never, ever* happen.

But she hesitated too long and her mom continued, "His family lives in Palos Verdes Estates and he has plans to go to Columbia University next year," she said, taking a sip of tea and watching Lola closely.

"Okay, and what does any of this have to do with me?" Lola asked calmly, trying to hide her mounting panic. "I mean, why do *I* have to meet him?" As far as Lola was concerned, she wasn't feeling very single right now, despite the fact that she'd just been dumped.

"Because I think it's important."

Lola took a deep breath and stared at her mother. She knew what this was about. Her mother had obviously found a nice Mexican boy who came from a good (i.e., wealthy, i.e., respectable) family, and she had absolutely no regard for the fact that Lola had recently had her heart *ripped to shreds* and wasn't exactly interested in meeting *anyone* right now. Okay, maybe her mom didn't know any of that because she hadn't exactly told her, but still. How could she do this to her?

"It's a shame you had to leave early to take your friend home," her mom continued, giving Lola a look that said she hadn't bought the story for one measly second. "Anyway, you should hear from him today or tomorrow. And Lola, when he asks you out, I expect you to say yes."

Lola just stood there, staring at her mother, knowing there was no way to win this one.

chapter twenty-four

Jade sat on her beach towel observing her friends. Anne was out there with Chris, doing surprisingly well. And according to Jade's unofficial count, Anne fell off Chris's longboard only a handful of times, which was pretty amazing for her very first day. But then again, it also seemed like Chris had found like a million reasons to hold on to her—like, way more than necessary.

Then there was Ellie, not doing much of anything but bobbing in the water, trying to act like she wasn't watching Chris and Anne, even though it was totally obvious that she was completely obsessed. Even from the vantage point of her towel, Jade could see Ellie's head swiveling around, watching their every move. *She must be feeling pretty lousy right about now,* Jade thought, remembering her friend's surprising behavior the night before. If it were anybody else, it wouldn't even be worth remembering. That's what parties were for! But Ellie wasn't just anybody—she held herself to a pretty impossible standard and up until last night, she'd managed to stick to it.

But it was Duncan that Jade really felt sorry for. Especially when he'd figure out that Ellie wasn't into him, that she was just using him to get back at Chris. Jade knew that Duncan had been crushing on Ellie for about as long as Ellie had been crushing on Chris. It was just so damn obvious that she couldn't understand why nobody else could see it.

She applied more sunscreen and lip balm, then lay back on her towel, closing her eyes against the sun. *Why is it so hard for people to stop lying to themselves?* she wondered.

"Hey, Jade." Lola dropped her towel right next to hers.

"What's up?" Jade peered at her friend, knowing for sure that something was definitely not going right in her life.

Lola just shrugged and dug through her beach bag, pulling out a stack of magazines that could stock an entire newsstand— *ELLEgirl, InStyle, Latina, SG, Teen Vogue, Vanity Fair, People, Shop Etc., Lucky* . . .

"Your bag must weigh thirty pounds," Jade laughed, reaching for one. "*House & Garden?*"

"Hey, I'm an addict. Any glossy will do," Lola said, putting on a straw cowboy hat to shade her face from the sun. "Oh, and have I mentioned that my mother has expanded her parental duties?"

"Oh no," Jade said. Lola's mother gave new meaning to the word "ambitious."

"Oh yes." Lola nodded. "She's now appointed herself as my very own dating director slash life coach."

"No way." Jade stared at her friend.

"Apparently she has a wonderful young man all lined up for me. So I now have the pleasure of sitting by my cell, breathlessly awaiting a call from *Diego*—the best thing to come out of Mexico City since my dad." She rolled her eyes dramatically and lay back on her towel. "Little does she know, I put my phone on vibrate so I won't have to hear it ring. He can just leave a message for all I care."

"Oh, that does not sound promising," Jade said, looking at her friend with sympathy. "But maybe it won't be as bad as you think."

Lola opened one eye and looked at her. "Jade, you've met my mother. I think we both know how bad it will be!"

"Oh, you know I hate negative thoughts, but this time you're probably right," she agreed.

"My life is a disaster." Lola shook her head and placed her hat completely over her face. "Tell you what, I'll just lie here with my eyes closed and you tell me if you see or read anything interesting. I just need to zone out for a while, but I swear I'm listening."

"Something interesting . . . Okay, well, my across-the-street neighbor keeps walking up and down the beach. This is now her fourth or fifth lap."

"Maybe she's just exercising," Lola said from under her hat.

"No, I think it's more about showing off her new boobs—those don't come cheap, you know. Okay, and Chris and Anne have been in the water for a while now, he's teaching her to surf, and believe it or not, she's actually pretty good. So good, in fact, that he probably does not need to be holding her quite as much as he is, which indicates something else entirely."

"What?"

"That Chris is totally into Anne," Jade said, impatiently.

"Chris and Anne?" Lola asked, removing her hat and opening one eye.

"Yup. So much for my big plans." Jade sighed and looked back toward the water.

"What plans?" Lola looked at her.

"Nothing," Jade said quickly, not wanting to share with Lola how she'd failed miserably at her own lame matchmaking attempt.

"Okay, continue. This is getting good," Lola said, replacing her hat.

"Okay, and poor Ellie has been bobbing out there for what must be hours now."

"Bobbing? Not surfing?" Lola's voice sounded muffled from beneath the straw.

"Not surfing. She's through with surfing. Well, at least for today. And it appears that her coach has abandoned her."

"Should we swim out there and talk to her?"

"No." Jade shook her head. "I have a feeling she just wants to be left alone. And Lola, I hate to break it to you, but your bag is vibrating."

chapter twenty-five

Realizing her fingers and toes were completely shriv-
eled from way too many hours spent in the water, Ellie hopped
on her board and rode her last, and possibly best, wave of the
day.

Dragging her board up the beach, she stopped to watch three
little tow-headed kids bury their father in the sand.

"Hey, Ellie!"

She looked over to see Jade, Lola, Anne, and Chris lying on
their towels, laughing and talking. Seeing Anne and Chris like
that, with their towels pushed so close together, made her stomach go all weird again. But now that they'd seen her she had no
choice but to go over and say a quick hello.

"Hey," she said, giving a little wave.

"How'd the coach work out?" Chris asked.

Ellie dropped her board on the sand and shrugged. "I guess I
just wasn't feeling very into it today."

"Maybe Anne could help you." He laughed. "She's a natural."

Ellie narrowed her eyes at him. He was so nice and easygoing
that he probably meant nothing by it, but still. *What a thing to say.*
Guys could be so insensitive.

"I doubt that. I've seen you surf," Anne said, looking at Ellie and smiling. "You're pretty amazing out there."

"When did you see me?" Ellie asked, wondering if Anne was spying on her or something, even though she knew how ridiculous that seemed.

"Um, early in the morning. Before school sometimes." Anne gave an embarrassed shrug.

"You get up at five thirty?" Ellie looked at her skeptically.

"Well, sometimes, yeah. I mean, when I can't sleep. I guess I'm still on East Coast time or something."

"I think you just found your new surf partner," Lola said. Then, looking at Anne she explained, "We all used to surf before school, but then Jade and I kind of dropped out. Unlike Ellie, we need our beauty sleep." She laughed.

"Speak for yourself!" Jade said, tossing her long brown ringlets and giving Lola a fake offended look.

"Well, I'm pretty serious about surfing, so I'm not really looking for company," Ellie said, feeling completely annoyed with her friends for pushing this girl on her. Why couldn't everyone just leave things the way they were?

"We're all thinking about going down to Taco Loco in a while. You wanna come?" Chris asked, grabbing Anne's water bottle and taking a sip.

Ellie just stood there, watching them. Their knees were bumping against each other, and the way he had just grabbed her water, so casually, almost like they were boyfriend and girlfriend or something. But that was impossible. *They just met!* "Um, no thanks," she said, grabbing her board and turning to leave. "I gotta be somewhere in half an hour."

"Where you going?" Jade called after her.

"Just somewhere," Ellie said, waving over her shoulder and heading toward home.

• • •

Walking up the beach stairs, she could feel her face grow hot. She was angry with her friends for totally not getting that she had no interest in hanging with Anne, not to mention how humiliating it was to watch her so effortlessly succeed at everything Ellie had worked so hard for. It's like she'd just come out of nowhere and within one week she'd moved in on Ellie's friends and Ellie's fantasy boyfriend, and now she was even showing a certain amount of skill at Ellie's sport.

She'd been watching her the whole time, and unfortunately Chris was right. Anne *was* a pretty good surfer. Maybe not good in the way that Ellie or Chris or even Jade or Lola was, but good in the way that if she got out there a couple times a week and really focused, she could definitely compete someday, and that was something that Ellie did not need. It was bad enough losing Chris to her; she certainly didn't need to lose Surf Fest, too.

Leaning her board against the wall, she threw her damp towel over a deck chair and went into the kitchen.

"Hey." Her brother was sitting at the table drinking a juice and reading last weekend's *L.A. Times* Calendar section.

"Did you just wake up?" she asked, realizing she sounded bossy and judgmental just like her dad, *but jeez,* it was three o'clock already.

"Out last night. Got home late," Dean said in that shorthand way of talking he had. He was all about word economy.

"Where?" Ellie asked, opening the fridge and looking for something to eat. All that time in the water had left her ravenous. *Too bad I can't go to Taco Loco,* she thought, grabbing a container of yogurt, determined to make do.

"Party. Monarch Beach," he said, still not looking up.

"Oh, I was at one at Aliso," she said, grabbing a spoon.

"So I heard."

"What do you mean?" she asked, panicked that word was out about her drinking three beers and making out with Duncan. Any other girl doing that would be no big deal, but Ellie idolized her brother and she wanted him to think well of her.

"Duncan called like an hour ago." He shrugged.

"What did he say?" she asked, hoping she sounded calm and casual.

"He wants you to call him." He looked up briefly.

"Did he say anything else?"

"No."

"So who was at the party?" she asked, determined to move the conversation away from herself. She did not want to think about Duncan right now.

"Some friends, some poseurs, the usual crowd." He shrugged, folded the paper in half, and looked at her.

Dean was pretty intolerant of poseurs, the kind of people who offered nothing more than their money and their presence. He, on the other hand, had accomplished so much in such a short amount of time, having won several surf championships with several major brands clamoring to sponsor him; he'd even gotten an early acceptance into a really good school. Yet despite his good looks and undeniable talents, he somehow managed to stay really low-key, often using his free time for community service, like assisting in beach cleanups or teaching autistic kids to surf or working on his ongoing surf documentary. But Ellie knew that his most amazing accomplishment to date was when he'd convinced their dad that taking the semester off school to work on his film was a genius idea. Ellie couldn't even take a sick day without getting seriously scolded. And as much as she loved Dean, sometimes it was a total bummer having a brother like him. He was a tough act to follow.

"Do you know what time Dad's coming home?" she asked, finishing her yogurt and dumping the container in the trash.

"Not 'til late." He looked at her and smiled. He knew just how hard their dad had been on her over the last few years.

"Good," she said, heading upstairs to her room so she could shower, change, and then head out to her secret place. She was looking forward to a little peace and quiet.

chapter twenty-six

Lola was staring at her half-eaten taco, impatiently waiting for Jade to take her home, even though all the immediate evidence suggested that was not about to happen anytime soon.

Impatiently chewing on the end of the straw she'd used to drink not one, but two Diet Cokes, she watched as Jade joked around with Ben and some older guys who were apparently friends of his that Lola had never seen before. Chris and Anne had taken off an hour ago, and Lola was beginning to wish she'd gone with them.

What a waste, she thought. Five single guys less than five feet away and things had gotten so bad for her that she didn't feel like flirting with any of them. But even worse was the fact that her phone hadn't rung all day. Not that she thought *he* would call. But still, it would have been nice.

But wait. Hadn't Jade told her on the beach that her bag was vibrating? She'd assumed at the time that it was that loser guy her mom was trying to hook her up with. *But what if it wasn't? What if he really did try to call?*

Anxiously, she reached into her bag, grabbing her cell and flipping it open, only to find a little envelope on the screen.

So she *had* gotten a message!

Excitedly, she pressed the voice-mail button, holding her breath and closing her eyes, anticipating the sound of his voice.

"Hi. My name's Diego. Apparently our parents think it's a good idea for us to meet. So if you want, you can give me a call back at . . ."

She erased it before he could finish. *Of course,* she thought, shaking her head and rolling her eyes. Well, there was no way she'd be calling him back. And when her mother asked, well, she'd just tell her that he never called. Because the one thing she knew for sure was that there was absolutely no way she was going out with him. No way in hell, *because only the most terminal dweeb would need his mother to set him up on a date!*

"Hey, Lola, you awake?" Jade asked, laughing and tapping her friend on the shoulder.

"Yeah, what's up?" she said, brushing her hair away from her face, hoping Jade was finally ready to bail.

"We're gonna go over to Tom's. Are you in?"

"Who's Tom?" Lola asked, squinting at the guys, unable to remember any of their names, which was so unlike her.

"Curly blond hair in the blue T-shirt, standing next to Mike who you also probably don't remember. Anyway, his apartment is just up the street. We're just gonna hang out, listen to some music . . ."

But before Jade could list all the activities that could be had at Tom's, Lola was already shaking her head. She knew they were all just gonna go back and smoke some pot, and Lola just wasn't into all that. What she really wanted was to be by herself for a while and just try to sort out all the conflicting emotions in her head. She needed a little downtime, she needed to chill, but she didn't need to do it at Tom's. "I don't think so," she said. "I think I'm gonna head home. Do you mind?" she asked, assuming Jade would go with her and feeling bad about wrecking her good time, but really, Jade didn't need to be hanging out with a bunch of older guys, either. *Oh great, now I'm even starting to think like Ellie,* she thought.

"No worries. Just take these, and leave it in the driveway," Jade said, handing her the car keys.

And before Lola could even respond, Jade was already walking down the street with Ben and his four stoner friends.

chapter twenty-seven

"See, the main difference between diving and surfing is the control issue. Like diving is all about perfect form, being in complete control of your body, and getting the moves just exactly right. But in surfing, yeah, okay, you have to be skilled enough to control your board as well as your body, but there's not just one specific way of doing it. Everyone brings their own unique experience to it. No one can tell you how to surf a wave. It's, like, as individual as your fingerprint," Chris said.

"That's the *only* difference?" Anne laughed, leaning into him. "'Cause I can think of like a million more."

"I said it's the *main* difference, not the *only* difference." He smiled.

They were sitting on her front lawn. Chris had his hands wrapped around his knees and Anne had her long, tanned legs splayed out in front of her, and they were both enjoying each other's company so much, it was pretty obvious neither of them wanted it to end.

They'd spent the entire day together, but there were still so many things to talk about. And Anne realized she hadn't been this happy since she'd left Connecticut. Then, when she looked up and saw Chris smiling at her, she was pretty sure she hadn't been this happy then, either.

"Maybe we should get a pizza and rent a movie," he said, stretching out his legs and lying back on the grass.

"After two tacos, two Cokes, nachos, Spanish rice, and refried beans?" she said, wrapping her arms around her full belly. "I don't think so. I'll burst if I eat anything else." She laughed.

"You're right," he said, sitting up abruptly and looking embarrassed. "I should bail. You're probably getting pretty sick of me by now." He looked embarrassed.

"I said I was *full*." She smiled. "I didn't say I was *bored*."

And then, mustering every last ounce of courage (since she'd never been one to make the first move), she closed her eyes, leaned in, and kissed him.

chapter twenty-eight

Ellie had been painting for hours, and now her fingers felt stiff, her back ached from standing for so long, and the light was beginning to fade so fast she could barely see her canvas. She flexed her fingers, trying to warm them up and get them limber again, then leaned over, opened her paint box, and began loading up her supplies.

She loved going to Treasure Island Park and being surrounded by all the other artists. She didn't know any of them personally, and most days there were several she'd never seen before, but there were always a few regulars she looked forward to seeing. Like the older woman with the long gray braid who painted with such bold, abstract strokes that Ellie couldn't tell if it was supposed to be the scenery in front of her or a more complicated landscape that existed only in her head. And the big, burly guy who looked like a Hell's Angel but painted in the most fragile, delicate, precise way. And then there were the wannabe bohemians, with their designer tote bags and expensive white linen shirts, who scowled in frustration when the task turned out to be much more difficult than they'd imagined. Ellie had watched more than a few of those types pack it up after ten minutes and head back to their suite at the Montage. For some people, she guessed, it was more the romantic idea of painting than the actual reality of it that was so intriguing.

Ellie had been coming here for years, but nobody knew about it. Nobody even knew she could paint—well, except for her mother, who had encouraged her daughter's natural artistic abilities ever since she was a small child, often walking her through the many downtown Laguna Beach galleries while Dean was at school.

One of Ellie's most cherished memories was of the time she and her mother visited the Getty Museum in Los Angeles, just weeks before her death. They'd spent the entire day there, exploring the grounds, enjoying a long lunch, and staring in wonder at some of the finest works of art. Ellie's mom had been thin and bald and easily exhausted from the months of chemo she'd endured, but with a colorful silk scarf tied around her head and her vintage jeans belted tightly around her waist, she'd grabbed Ellie's hand and forged ahead, determined to ignore the curious stares of others and just enjoy her last days.

But Ellie's father knew nothing of her painting. He had so little appreciation for art that Ellie was sure he could never understand how important it was to her. And even though her friends would definitely be supportive, the truth was, it was kind of nice to have something totally private that belonged only to her.

She was pretty good, too. Or at least she suspected she might be. Every now and then one of the regulars would pass by and say, "Looks nice." Or, "You really captured those wildflowers."

Of course, it was possible that they were just being kind, but there was a small part of her, deep down inside, that was convinced there really was something there.

The funny thing was that her secret place was just a short five-minute drive from Laguna Cove, yet nobody would ever think to look for her here. Which made it all the more perfect.

It was like being able to hide in plain view.

• • •

Driving through the Laguna Cove gate, she was waving at the guard just as her cell phone rang. Not recognizing the number on the display, she contemplated letting it go to voice mail, but Ellie was nothing if not dependable, and reliable, and she just wasn't capable of not answering a ringing phone.

"Hello?" she said, cautiously.

"Ellie? It's Duncan."

"Oh, hey." She rolled her eyes, wishing she'd never picked up. Oh well, she'd have to tell him sooner or later, so it may as well be now.

"Sorry to keep calling, I guess I was just a little worried about you. You didn't sound so hot this morning," he said, laughing nervously.

"I wasn't," she admitted, turning onto her street. "But I'm better now."

"Good. Um, Ellie, I was wondering." He paused.

Oh God, here it comes, she thought, cringing as though something was about to fly through the windshield and smack her in the face.

"Would you want to go out sometime? I mean, like to dinner or something?" He sounded so nervous, it made her feel awful.

"Duncan, I . . ." She hesitated. She'd turned down plenty of guys before so what was the big deal now? *Maybe it was because you totally made out with him, and led him on,* she thought, shaking her head at her own lack of control. "I just think . . ." She slowed down as she passed by Anne's house, which was right next to hers.

Oh my God! Is that Anne and Chris? MAKING OUT ON THE FRONT LAWN? She adjusted her rearview mirror, just to make sure.

"You just think what?" Duncan asked.

"Sorry, what?" Ellie said, pulling into her driveway, completely distracted, yet still gawking at the house next door. Apparently things were moving along a lot quicker than even she had imagined possible.

"I just asked you out, and you were about to answer me," he said. He was beginning to sound annoyed.

"Oh, right. Sorry." She couldn't help it. She had to look again. It was dark, but it was definitely them. They'd even lit up the motion sensor lights. Which meant they were both moving around. *Oh, God.*

"Listen, if you're not interested, it's totally cool," he said, definitely sounding like he didn't actually think it was so cool.

"Um, Duncan? Actually I'd love to go out with you," she said, shocked to hear herself actually saying the words, but somehow it just felt right. Then, taking control, as always, she asked, "So what are you doing tonight?"

chapter twenty-nine

Lola sat at the dinner table with her mother and *Abuela. So much for time alone, lying in bed, wallowing in heartache,* she thought.

"So, did he call you yet?" *Abuela* asked, eyes shining with anticipation.

Oh, great, now all the generations are in on it. Well, that just wouldn't do. "Who?" Lola asked innocently, cutting into the grilled sea bass on her plate.

"The boy! What's his name?" She looked at her daughter-in-law.

"Diego. Diego Martinez," Lola's mom said, looking right at Lola.

"So?" *Abuela* nodded, as though ready to hear the world's greatest love story.

But Lola just shook her head. "Nope, not a peep," she told her, reaching for her glass of iced tea. She wasn't a very good liar, even though she found herself doing it more and more these days.

"I can't believe this! I've never heard of such a thing!" *Abuela* said, sounding personally affronted that the very desirable Diego had dissed her precious granddaughter. "Who does he think he is?"

Lola looked up to see *Abuela* glaring at her daughter-in-law, as though it was *her* fault he hadn't called, and she knew she had to say something. Their relationship was strained enough as it is. "I had my phone on 'vibrate' all day, so maybe I missed it." She shrugged, hoping this compromise would be good enough to hold them over until she could think of something better.

"You kids and your cell phones," *Abuela* said, shaking her head.

Add that to the list of modern conveniences that aren't to be trusted, Lola thought. *Along with microwaves, computers, iPods*—although she sure learned to love that flat-screen TV.

"I really think it would be good if you two could meet before the cotillion next month. I think he'd make the perfect escort for your debut," her mother said.

My debut? Like I'm an actress or a novelist? Lola had no interest in cotillions, high society, or just about anything else her mother held dear. Where was her father when she needed him? *Oh, that's right. Working, as always.* She shook her head. She'd had enough— enough dinner and enough of this conversation. "Well, it's really not up to me if he calls or not, now is it?" she said, looking from her mother to her grandmother. Then, getting up, she excused herself from the table and headed down the hall.

When she got to her room she stripped off her clothes, slipped into some red silk pajamas, and crawled between the sheets. It was just seven forty-five on a Saturday night and she was already in bed. That's what her pathetic life had come to.

She rolled onto her side and stared at her creamy white walls, wondering what *he* was doing, and if he felt sad, too.

Or if, maybe, he'd barely even thought about her. Maybe he'd already moved on.

chapter thirty

Jade was lying on the couch, with her bare feet propped up on a pile of overstuffed cushions while her head rested on Ben's lap as he raked his fingers through her long, curly hair. Everything about being with Ben just felt so calm, peaceful, and free, and she thought how lucky she was to have a guy friend like this. One that you could just hang with, and not have to have it get all romantic and complicated. She hated when relationships got complicated.

"My dad's driving down tomorrow," Ben said, gazing down at her and rubbing her temples with his thumbs. "He wants to have lunch, so he can explain his side, but I'm not so sure I want to hear it."

"You should go. At least listen to what he has to say," Jade said, looking up at him.

"I don't know." He shook his head. "I think he's just gonna give me a bunch of crap about how hard he's got it. Even though he's the one who chose to leave." He looked at her.

Jade just nodded. They'd talked about his parents' divorce before and it was basically the same old story. Dad has an affair, Mom finds out, Dad vacates, taking most of the money, Mom works two jobs to provide the basics, and the kids feel abandoned by everyone. *Why can't people just be nicer to each other?* she thought. *What's with all the greed?*

"It's your call," she said, unwilling to judge his decisions. "But if you give him a chance and he fails, well then, at least you took the high road, right?"

Ben shrugged. "It's just, everything is so much more complicated now. My mom's totally overworked and depressed, and I don't know, sometimes I just feel like maybe I should bail on school and get a job so I can help her. Or maybe I should just move out. You know, go somewhere and do my own thing, so she won't have to worry about supporting me anymore."

Jade sat up abruptly and looked at him. "You can't quit school! That's like, a one-way ticket to Loserville! I mean, who's that gonna help? Certainly not your mother, and definitely not you," she said, hoping he was just being dramatic and wasn't actually serious.

Ben gave her a surprised look. "Okay, so tell me how you really feel."

"I'm serious. And don't look at me like that. I'm actually very practical." She smiled.

Ben glanced around the room and then back at Jade. "Hey, you wanna bail?" he asked, standing up abruptly.

"What? Now?" she asked, wondering why he was suddenly acting so anxious and strange. Just five minutes ago everything had been so mellow and perfect.

"Listen, you can hang if you want, but I really need to get some fresh air," he said, heading straight for the door.

"Hey, wait up! I'll go with you," she said, grabbing her purse and hurrying to catch up with him.

chapter thirty-one

"I'm just not sure how much longer I can get away with this," Lola said, climbing out of Ellie's car and reaching for her book bag. "I mean, he's left two messages now and it's just a matter of time before my mom finds out I'm ignoring his calls."

"How will she know?" Ellie asked, clicking her car alarm and glancing around nervously for Duncan. Not seeing him anywhere, she relaxed and focused her attention back on her friend.

"We're talking about *my mom*. She has ways of finding out *everything*. I swear, sometimes I wonder if she has a secret life as a spy or something." Lola laughed, half joking but half serious as well.

"Have you talked to Jade?" Ellie asked. "I tried calling her a few times on Sunday, but I couldn't find her."

"Haven't seen her." Lola shook her head. "I surfed a little in the afternoon with Chris and Anne; then we all went for smoothies at the Shake Shack."

Ellie stopped, right in the middle of the student parking lot, and stared at Lola. "You hung out with Chris and Anne?" she asked, feeling her face go all red but unable to stop it.

"Yeah." Lola looked more than a little confused by Ellie's reaction.

"Are they like, *a couple now*? I mean, like boyfriend and girlfriend?" Ellie felt her throat go all tight.

"I'm not sure I want to put a label on it," Lola said, tugging on Ellie's arm. "Come on, you're gonna make us late."

Ellie reluctantly followed Lola. "I just don't get what you all see in this Anne chick. I mean, what's so special about her? She seems pretty ordinary to me, yet you guys act like she's *so great*."

"She's actually pretty nice. And I really think you should cut her some slack, give her a chance."

"I don't trust her." Ellie looked right at Lola. "And I'm not sure you should, either."

"What's that supposed to mean?" Lola asked, sounding slightly annoyed.

"I mean, what do we really know about her? *Nothing!* And if you think about it, it's like, she just came here out of nowhere and already she's dating Chris, learning to surf, and you guys are all totally falling for it! You're totally hanging out with her!"

"It's called making friends and fitting in. And you really need to relax. Just think how she feels. Having to move all the way across the country and trying to fit in somewhere new. *Especially* here! People around here can be pretty exclusive, you know," Lola said, shooting her friend a look.

"What's that supposed to mean?" Ellie asked, folding her arms in front of her and sounding really defensive.

But Lola just shrugged.

"Well, I'm only saying you shouldn't go around trusting *everyone*. And I'm more than a little hurt that you could find the time to surf with *her* and not with *me*," Ellie said.

Lola took a deep, exasperated breath. "Look, for one thing, it's not like it was o' dark hundred, like when you're ready to surf. It was a normal time, for normal people. And for another, you seriously need to lighten up."

"*Normal people?*" Ellie just stood there looking at her. She couldn't believe Lola had just said that.

"Look, I'm sorry. But I've got my own problems right now and

I'm not going to do this with you, okay? Just try to loosen up a little, would you?" she said, turning and heading toward her locker.

Ellie stood there and watched her walk away. She knew she was acting crazy, possessive, out of control, and ridiculously jealous, but the problem was, she didn't know how to stop.

"Hey, El," Duncan said, approaching her with this huge grin on his face.

Ellie took one look at that smile and felt her heart sink. It was her fault he was so happy today. If she hadn't asked him out Saturday night, then he wouldn't be approaching her now. Well, he might be, but not like that. Not like he expected something. "Hey," she said, giving him a tight half smile.

"You have AP English now, right?" he said, as though he was all ready to walk her to class.

"Yeah, but I have to go to the restroom first, so you really don't have to wait for me. I'll see you at lunch, okay?" she said, feeling bad about the disappointed look on his face, but happy about the four-hour cushion between first period and lunch.

She headed toward the bathroom until she was sure he was no longer watching, then turned and went to class. She felt bad about blowing him off like that, because the truth was she *did* have fun with him Saturday night. They'd gone to dinner at a cozy little Thai restaurant and then they'd walked around some of the galleries in downtown Laguna, both surprising each other with their appreciation of art. And when he'd dropped her off at her door, she'd even let him kiss her again. And this time she was completely sober. *And,* she had to admit, it was pretty nice.

But still, he wasn't Chris. And by the time she was back in her room, changing for bed, she'd come to her senses, deciding that she definitely had to cut it off as soon as possible.

chapter thirty-two

Anne had initially set out to get back at Ellie, so she was pretty surprised when she found herself liking Chris as much as she did. *But what's not to like?* He was cute, smart, funny, sweet—she really couldn't find anything wrong with him. And the fact that he'd given her a ride to school (sparing her from being chauffeured by Jake), and then even walked her to class, kissing her briefly just outside the door, made her feel so happy and dreamy, *nothing* could get her down.

Until she saw Ellie glaring at her from across the room.

Anne just didn't get it. All of Ellie's friends were great, but no matter how hard she tried, Ellie refused to give her a chance. And Anne was getting tired of trying. Yet she also couldn't stand to keep things the way they were.

Taking her seat, she glanced at Lola and Ellie and waved. Lola smiled and waved back, but Ellie turned her head abruptly and stared straight ahead at the chalkboard, even though it was completely blank. The whole thing was so ridiculous that Anne almost felt sorry for her. Almost.

After roll call, Mr. Campbell leaned on the edge of his desk and, opening his book, said, "Anne, would you read the beginning of chapter two for us?"

They were reading *The Great Gatsby,* one of Anne's very favorite books. She loved it so much, she'd even rented the movie version once. But even though Robert Redford used to be a complete and total hottie, it just didn't compare to the book. And now, even though she'd read the story many times before, she finally felt like she could totally relate to Gatsby. Because now she knew just how hard it was to try to fit in.

She just hoped things would work out a little better for *her* than they did for *him.*

She cleared her throat and began reading. When she was well into the third paragraph, Mr. Campbell said, "Okay stop right there. Can anyone tell me the significance of Dr. T. J. Eckleburg?"

"Well," Anne said, feeling excited that she knew the answer and not realizing Ellie already had her hand in the air. "He symbolizes God, and the valley of ashes is like, purgatory, because later in the book . . ."

"Excuse me, Mr. Campbell, but we haven't exactly finished the book, have we? We're only on chapter two. And maybe some of us don't want to know how it ends just yet," Ellie said, glaring at Anne and shaking her head.

Anne looked at Mr. Campbell, her face turning red.

"Well, you have a point, Ellie. Though, without giving away too much, you'll see as you continue reading that the eyes are symbolic of God, and the valley does become a place filled with violence and grief. Now Harrison, would you continue reading where Anne left off?"

And as Anne listened to Harrison read, she looked across the room at Ellie. *That was the last time you get to humiliate me,* she thought as their eyes briefly met.

chapter thirty-three

By Thursday, when Ben still hadn't shown up at
school, Jade was starting to freak. "You guys, what if he really did
run away?" she asked, hugging her knees against her chest and
shaking her head. "I have to find him."

"Whoa, wait a second. I mean, why don't you just call his house
and see if he's home?" Ellie said, squeezing salt water out of her
hair and twisting it into a bun.

"Thanks, Kojak." Jade rolled her eyes. She loved Ellie, yeah, but
sometimes she so didn't get it. "Believe me, I already tried that.
Nobody answers."

"But you said his mom works two jobs, so she's probably never
there," Lola said. "Did you go by his house?"

"Nobody home. Even Tom and those guys don't know where
he is. You guys so don't get it. I'm really worried, and I feel like
I've got to do something. I can't just sit around here and wait," she
said, getting up from her towel.

"You're right, I don't get it. Are you guys like, dating?" Ellie asked,
putting on SPF 30 even though the sun would soon be fading.

"No, we're not dating, but he is my friend and I care about him.
Just like I'd care if it were one of you," Jade said, shaking her
head. Okay, maybe they'd seen her try to rescue one too many

strays before, but this time it wasn't some lost kitten, or lonely rabbit. This time, it was serious.

"Well, maybe he's at his dad's," Lola said cautiously.

"Doubtful." Jade stood in front of her friends, curls blowing like crazy in the breeze. "He's pretty pissed at him right now, so it's not likely they're spending any quality time together. I just don't get why he hasn't called me."

"Typical. The ones you want to call never do." Lola shook her head sadly. Then, noticing her friends were staring, she said, "What? It's totally true."

"There's a guy out there who hasn't called you?" Ellie asked, laughing.

"You'd be surprised." Lola shrugged ruefully.

"Uh, hello? Back to me and my crisis," Jade said, waving her hands around to get their attention. Did they think this was a *joke*?

"Sorry, Jade. Go on," Ellie said; Lola nodded.

"Okay, so the other night after we left Tom's we took a ride up into the canyon, and we parked the car and just talked for hours. He's really upset about his parents splitting up, and he's not entirely rational right now. He was even talking about dropping out of school and stuff. I tried to explain how crazy that would be, but he was kind of messed up and I guess I wasn't able to really communicate with him like I wanted. He left me a message Sunday night, and that's the last I heard."

"Well, what'd he say in the message?" Lola asked.

"Nothing, really. But at the end he said, 'See you Monday.'"

"I don't think you should get involved, Jade. I'm sorry, but I don't. You've done everything you can, and I'm sure his mom has a handle on it. You can't save everyone, you know," Ellie said gently.

"Maybe not, El. But the least I can do is try." Jade grabbed her towel and headed toward the beach stairs.

"Jade! Wait, where you going?" Lola called after her.

"Back to Tom's. I have to start somewhere," she said.

chapter thirty-four

Anne was loving her new life—*What's not to love,* she thought. She had a great house with a private beach, she'd made good friends, and she had the most amazing boyfriend *ever.*

At least she thought he was her boyfriend. It's not like the actual words were ever spoken or anything. But they did spend a lot of time together, and she was pretty sure he was beginning to like her just as much as she liked him.

Oh yeah, and she'd finally found a sport she was as passionate about as diving. At first, she admitted, learning to surf was all about spending time with Chris. But now she loved it so much she found herself getting up early in the morning and heading out on her own. Usually she ran into Ellie, but Anne had finally learned to ignore her. There was nothing else she could do. She'd tried being quiet, she'd tired being nice—nothing worked. And it seemed like the more she hung with Chris and the better she got at surfing, the more Ellie glared at her. But that was Ellie's problem, and she was just gonna have to get used to coexisting in the same neighborhood, the same school, and with the same group of friends. Because now that Anne had found her place, she wasn't about to budge.

In fact, Anne was getting so good at surfing that just the other day Chris had mentioned Surf Fest to her.

"I can't compete! I'm just a beginner, I'll make a total fool of myself!" she'd said, shaking her head vehemently.

"True. There's no way you'll win, since there will be people there who grew up on surfboards. But it's such a cool contest, and it's open to everyone. If nothing else, just think of it as good practice, and a chance for you to get out there and see what it's like," he told her.

"Why can't I just go as an observer?" she'd asked. "You know, sit back and watch from the comfort of my very own beach chair?"

"That's not how it works. No one learns from just watching. You have to experience it to really know it. Besides, don't you miss competing?" he'd asked, leaning over to kiss her.

They were out in the water, sitting on their boards. "I have to think about it," she'd said, leaning toward him.

But ever since he'd brought up the idea, she'd been thinking about it more and more. He was right. She did miss competing. She missed the preparation before a big event, the nervous stomach the night before, and the thrill of scoring the highest at the end of the day. Okay, so she probably wouldn't be scoring the highest at Surf Fest. She probably wouldn't even come close. But hey, she had to start *somewhere*.

She opened the door to her giant walk-in closet, staring at the racks of clothes and wondering what she should wear. The wrap party for her dad's film was tonight and she'd invited all of her friends. She had a feeling that even Ellie might show. Not that she'd invited her, but she had invited Duncan and it kind of seemed like they were dating or something. Actually, it was hard to tell exactly what their deal was. While it was obvious that Duncan was totally into it, Ellie on the other hand always seemed like she was just along for the ride. But Anne knew better than to discuss it with Jade and Lola. Those three went way back, and Anne had no doubt where their loyalties lay.

But it would be a big party, with a ton of people, so she was sure it would be just as easy to ignore Ellie there as it was at school.

Slipping into her favorite jeans, a beaded cami, and some silver flats, she grabbed her purse and was heading for the living room to wait for Chris when Jake walked in.

"Oh my God, you scared me," Anne said, not expecting to see him. "What're you doing here? Aren't you going to the party?"

"I had to pick up some stuff for your dad. I'm headed up that way in a little while if you need a lift," he offered.

"No thanks, I've got a ride. You're not wearing that, are you?" she asked, realizing she sounded like a bitch, *but still*. Even by laid-back Hollywood standards, she doubted he should be showing up in his usual old shredded flip-flops, faded board shorts, and a holey T-shirt.

"Jeez, you're brutal," he said, laughing good-naturedly. "Of course I'm not wearing this. I do have other clothes, you know." He shook his head and walked down the hall toward the spare room where he kept some of his stuff.

Anne sat on the couch, trying to focus on the TV and not on her watch. It was so unlike Chris to be late, and now nearly twenty minutes had passed since he was supposed to pick her up. She went over to the window, pulled the drapes back, and checked the driveway—nothing, *nada. Should I call him?* she wondered. *Or would that seem overbearing? If he shows up right now, should I act cool, like I hadn't even noticed he was way late? Or should I stand my ground until I get an explanation?*

She shook her head and went back to the couch. What *was* with her? She'd never acted so ridiculous over a guy before. Or had she? She tried remembering what she'd been like when she first started going out with Justin, but so much had happened since then, the memory was foggy at best. Oh God, maybe she was turning into her mother—seemingly cool and confident on the outside, but a total emotional dependent on the inside. It was too horrible to think about. And it was stupid. She should just pick up the phone and find out what was taking him so long.

The second she grabbed the receiver, it rang, startling her so much she dropped it on the floor. "Hello?" she said, frantically flipping it right side up.

"Anne?" It was Chris.

"Hey, where are you?" she asked.

"Um, I'm really sorry, but I'm running late," he said. "Is there any way I can meet you there?"

"Are you serious?" she asked, sitting on the arm of the couch. "I mean, is everything okay?"

"Yeah, everything's cool. It's just that I'm over at Ellie's and we're behind schedule, and I don't want you to miss out because of me."

"You're at *Ellie's*?" She could feel the panic rise in her throat. "What are you guys doing?"

"We're lab partners, and we started a new project today," he said, as though that explained everything.

Well, maybe it did. But like a typical guy, he was missing all the subtext! She imagined Ellie sitting next to him, listening in on the whole conversation, while a big fat evil smile spread slowly across her face . . .

"But you're still coming, right?" she said, trying to sound cool and not needy, since there was nothing cool about being needy.

"Definitely. See you in a few?"

"Um, yeah, great," she said, hanging up and feeling totally shell-shocked.

"You're still here?" Jake said, walking down the hallway. His hair was still damp from the shower and combed away from his face, and he was dressed in a pair of vintage-wash denim jeans and a shirt with blue, green, yellow, and white stripes, untucked with the sleeves rolled up. His feet were bare and he was carrying his shoes.

"Yeah," Anne said, looking at him and swallowing hard. What was wrong with her? One minute she was getting all freaked out over Chris, and the next she was practically drooling at how well Jake cleaned up. It was ridiculous. *She* was ridiculous. And it meant nothing! He'd just startled her, that's all. "Chris can't make it 'til later, so do you think you could give me a ride?" She bit down on her lower lip nervously and tried not to stare at him.

"I've got a full tank of gas and the passenger seat is empty, so follow me." He smiled and headed for the front door.

chapter thirty-five

Lola was in her room, standing in front of her mirror, completely hating her life. Wouldn't you just know it—on the one night she was finally getting over being dumped, finally looking forward to breaking loose and having a little fun with her friends, her mother had arranged for her to meet Diego. She had just gotten home from school and walked into the kitchen to grab a snack when her mother had totally ambushed her.

"I've arranged for you and Diego to meet at the party tonight," she said, smiling brightly.

Lola stuck her head in the fridge and counted to ten, but it didn't really help. "Mom, I don't want to meet him. I just wanna hang with my friends," she told her, grabbing an apple and turning to face her.

"'Want to,' Lola. Not 'wanna.' And Diego is going to be there anyway, so you may as well get to know him."

"But why?" Lola looked at her mom. She felt like stomping her feet and throwing a tantrum like a two-year-old. Because that's how they made her feel—like she was totally at their mercy, and had absolutely no control over her own life.

"I think you two are going to really hit it off. *And,* I might add,

I happen to know you've been ignoring his messages. I did not raise you to be so rude, Lola," she said, giving her a stern look. "Now, are you riding with us? Or are you going with your friends?"

"*You guys* are going, too?" *Oh, that's just great. Why don't they all just double-date? Wouldn't that be fun!*

"Of course we're going," her mother said impatiently.

"Then I'm getting a ride with my friends. I'm sure you, Dad, Diego, and I will have plenty of time to hang at the party," Lola said, taking a bite of her apple, stomping down the hall, and slamming her bedroom door, not caring for one second what the consequences of *that* might be. *It's not like it can get any worse,* she thought.

And now she had the fun task of finding something cool enough to wear to a glitzy Hollywood party that her parents would also approve of. *Talk about impossible.*

"Maybe you can, like, have a major blowout, but no one gets hurt," Lola said. She was sitting next to Duncan in his dad's brand-new Lexus convertible. Lola knew he'd scored the car to impress Ellie, so it was too bad she'd canceled on him at the very last minute.

"I don't think my dad would be too cool with that," Duncan said, glancing over at her briefly. "You probably shouldn't even wish things like that; we're just getting off the freeway, for God's sake." He shook his head.

"Easy for you to say. You have no idea what I'm in for. No idea of what my mom is even capable of."

"How bad can it be?" Duncan asked. "Is he like, a big geek or something?"

"Probably," Lola laughed. "But that's not the point. It's all about *information,* and how my parents are steadily infiltrating every single corner of my life. And if I'm not careful, then the Lolita that you know and love will quietly disappear, and all that remains will be Lola. And everyone knows what a bore she is." She rolled her eyes and looked out the window.

"I kind of like Lola," Duncan said, looking at her and smiling.

"You would," she laughed. Then, staring in disbelief as they pulled into the parking lot, she shrieked, "Oh my God, don't turn here, just keep going, keep going, oh no, it's too late, they've made us." Lola sighed and rolled her eyes. "Well, it's been nice knowing ya, Duncan." She climbed out of the car, waving reluctantly at her parents, who were standing next to the valet stand, obviously waiting for her arrival. "Oh, and Duncan, you will *never, ever* get to be my getaway driver, should I need one someday. You failed miserably at this little operation. Still, I would advise you to run fast and far from the crazy Latina in the overpriced dress over there," she said, pointing at her mother, completely oblivious to the fact that the miniskirt she'd worn in rebellion had folded up in such a way that you could almost see, well, *France.*

"Here's Lola now," her mother said, arranging her lips into a tight perfunctory smile while her disapproving eyes focused on Lola's hiked-up skirt, tiny cardigan, tinier tank top, and little ballet flats. "This is Diego," she said, as though presenting a masterpiece.

"Hey," Lola said, noticing his precisely styled and gelled dark brown hair—which he'd probably spent the last hour getting to look like he hadn't thought about it in weeks—and the perfectly groomed brows that put her own to shame. And was that? Could it be? Was he actually wearing just the tiniest hint of Smith's Rosebud Salve on his bottom lip?

"Hey." He smiled, showing off his perfect white game-show-host teeth.

He must be a model/actor, she thought. *He's too perfect to be anything else.*

"Well, I'm sure you two have lots to talk about!" her mother singsonged. "So we'll be on our way. Have fun!" She smiled tightly, while discreetly grabbing the hem of Lola's miniskirt and yanking it down as far as it would go.

chapter thirty-six

Okay, this was not at all how she imagined it would be. All day at school, when Anne had been playing the movie version of the party in her head (instead of listening to her teachers drone on and on about subjects that just couldn't compare), she had cast herself in the starring role, as the girl with all the best lines. She'd pictured herself dressed in an outfit she didn't actually own but had seen recently in *Teen Vogue*, making brilliant, outrageous comments that would make Chris laugh so hard, he would look her right in the eye and say, "I just love you, Anne." And then, stopping to catch his breath, he would reach for her hand, look deep into her eyes, and say, "Really. I think I'm falling in love with you." Then, as the camera zoomed in for a close-up of the lovely young couple embracing, the background music would swell into some really sappy love song (possibly titled "Anne's Theme"), which would make the entire audience reach for a tissue, gently dabbing at their eyes while smiling through their tears.

But not once, in her wildest fantasies, did this particular movie open with her getting ditched first by her date/almost boyfriend, who was working on a science project (she hoped it wasn't a *biology* experiment) with the Villain (every good screenplay had one). And then ditched a second time by her dad's little helper (who, for one insane and vulnerable moment in the living room, she had actually thought was quite gorgeous).

It was like the second they'd walked in the restaurant, Jake had grabbed a glass of champagne from a passing waiter, thrust it at Anne, and then hightailed it to the other side of the room, as far away as possible, leaving her standing in the corner, all alone, sipping champagne and looking like the world's biggest reject.

She pulled her cell phone out of her purse and checked to see if Chris had called and she'd somehow failed to hear it ring. But the second she glanced at the blank screen, she felt embarrassed for even looking. Because even though that very same act was probably being played out at that exact same moment by millions of girls across the globe, that didn't make it any less pathetic.

Shaking her head at her own lameness, she took another sip of champagne and looked across the room to see Jade and Ben. *Finally, someone to talk to,* she thought.

"Jade!" she yelled, waving her hands around like a desperate rescue victim, beyond caring about just how far from cool she was straying. "Hey, how long have you been here?" she asked, looking from Jade to Ben and noticing his eyes were all bloodshot as usual.

"Just arrived. Did we miss anything?" Jade asked.

"No, I've just been really busy warming up this wall." She shrugged. "I guess the big stars don't arrive until later. It's mostly just crew right now."

"Hey, where'd you get the bubbles?" Ben asked, looking at Anne's glass.

"One of the waiters. They're all over the place. And it's an open bar."

"Ben, maybe we should just hang for a while," Jade said, giving him a pleading look.

"I'm hanging." He looked at her and smiled. "I'd just rather be hanging with a drink in my hand. Anybody need anything?" he asked, heading toward the bar.

Anne shook her head. She knew she should just stick with the one glass—she didn't want to end up alone, embarrassed, and drunk.

Jade shook her head and watched him walk away. "I just don't know what else to do," she whispered, the second he was out of earshot.

"What do you mean?" Anne looked at her.

"Well, it's like, I'm totally trying to be a good friend, and I'm really trying to help, but it's like he doesn't even care what happens to him. Not to mention that he still won't tell me where he was all week, and he gets totally annoyed when I ask. I never should have brought him here. I don't think Ben and an open bar is such a good combination," she said, looking really worried.

Anne watched Ben push his way to the front of the line. "I'm sure it'll all be fine," she assured her. But deep down inside, she wondered if that was really true.

chapter thirty-seven

"So," Lola said, tapping her water bottle against Diego's. "It's *so great* to finally meet you."

But Diego just looked at her and smiled. "Is it?" he asked, raising his eyebrows.

"Well, yeah. I mean, I've heard so much about you, and stuff," Lola said, trying to come off as interested and enthusiastic even though she could feel herself losing steam. Now that he was directly in front of her she was determined to just play it out—by being nice and saying all the right things. Though he wasn't making it very easy for her. And something about the look on his face told her he wasn't buying her act for one measly second.

"Is that why you didn't return my calls? Because you'd heard *too much* about me? Or were you just playing hard to get?" he asked, giving her an amused look.

Lola focused on the white linen tablecloth, running her fingernails over it and wondering what to say next. For the first time in her entire life, she was completely clueless about how to act around a guy. Normally it was so instinctive with her, but this time it was totally different. And she wasn't sure if it was because her parents were involved in the setup or what. But it almost seemed like he was toying with her, and that he wasn't all that interested. Which was even more unusual. Had getting dumped made her unconsciously send out some kind of crazy pheromone that repelled men? Was that even *possible*? Or had she finally met the one guy who genuinely had no interest in her? And if so, then didn't that mean she was destined to fall in love with him?

But Lola was still dealing with lost love, and this guy, gorgeous as he was, just didn't seem like he could inspire those kinds of feelings in her. There was something different about him. Something she just couldn't put her finger on. "Um, well, you're right. It was really rude of me to ignore your message. And I'm sorry," she said, looking up at him briefly. "My parents don't exactly know this, but I was really into someone, and he just dumped me like the day before you called. So I guess I wasn't exactly into meeting someone new. In fact, you seem really nice and all, and you're definitely really good-looking and stuff, and your outfit is like *so hot,* but I have to be honest with you, I just can't date you right now. I mean, not just you, but *anyone*. I just need to be alone for a while. I hope you can understand," she said, focusing intently on the tablecloth and hoping he was taking it okay. She was afraid to look at him. She couldn't stand hurting anyone's feelings. "I mean, I don't want to lead you on, or anything."

When she finally did look up, Diego's dark brown eyes were all watery and his knuckles were turning white as he gripped the edge of the table. "Lola, stop. Please," he said, laughing so hard he was doubled over.

Well, it's not like she'd meant to be funny! She was just trying to let him down easy! She sat there staring at him, eyes narrowed, arms folded across her chest, waiting for an explanation.

When he finally calmed down, he looked at her and said, "Please, don't worry about it, okay? You're not exactly my type."

Not his type? What's that supposed to mean? And who the hell does he think he is, laughing at me like that? "Oh, well fine," she said, shrugging like she didn't care, like she wasn't the least bit offended. "I mean, I don't exactly get why that's *so damn funny,* but obviously you do." She stood up and adjusted her miniskirt, which had risen up again. She'd never been so humiliated. She was going to find her mother and make her pay for this.

"Lola, sit down please," he said.

"Um, no thanks. Although it's been a *real pleasure* meeting you." She rolled her eyes sarcastically.

"Lola, I'm sorry, really. Look, I didn't mean to offend you," he said, looking at her and motioning for her to sit. "There's a very good reason for what I just said."

She looked at him, hands on hips, waiting. *Oh, this ought to be good.*

"I'm gay." He looked at her and shrugged.

"You're *gay?*" she repeated, raising her eyebrows and giving him a skeptical look, wondering if he was just saying that. But as she slowly sank back down onto her chair, she once again noticed the perfect brows, the buffed nails, and the fact that he wasn't flirting with her. *Of course,* she thought. *Now it all makes sense.*

He leaned toward her and smiled, revealing a row of perfectly straight white teeth. "So tell me," he said. "Where did you get that outfit? It's genius."

chapter thirty-eight

Anne's eyes had been glued to the door for the past hour and a half, and she was really starting to hate herself for it. Here she was, at a wrap party full of some of the hottest stars (well, maybe not the *hottest*), and all she could think about was Chris and Ellie. It was totally pathetic, and she was really starting to get on her own nerves.

Jade had taken off in search of Ben, who had never quite made it back from the bar. *What on earth does a cute, optimistic, happy girl like Jade see in a big loser like Ben,* she wondered. Yeah, he had his share of problems, and Anne had firsthand knowledge of just how awful it can be when your parents decide to split. But it didn't really seem like he was even trying to make it better. If anything, it almost seemed like he was using it as an excuse to mess up.

Then there were Lola and Diego. They were sitting right across the table from her, but they were so incredibly wrapped up in each other, it was like they were having their own private party in the midst of this big one. Diego seemed nice enough, and he was certainly gorgeous, but it was still kind of weird to see Lola so worked up over someone her mom had set her up with. She'd always made it sound like her mom could introduce her to Orlando Bloom and she would find a valid reason to reject him. But now, against all odds, there they were, in their own little world, heads close together, talking a mile a minute. Go figure.

Then there was the situation with her dad. As if it wasn't weird enough to be hanging at the same party and being forced to realize that he was way more popular (and from the looks of it, having way more fun) than her, so far both times she'd run into him there'd been this mysterious pretty petite redhead permanently attached to his right arm.

Okay, maybe she wasn't all that mysterious, since her dad had introduced her as Brooke, and had also mentioned something about her working in makeup or wardrobe. *Or was it set design?* Anne couldn't specifically remember because she was way too freaked out by the fact that there even *was* a Brooke in his life. A Brooke who seemed way too comfortable hanging all over her dad and knew way too much about Anne. Were they a *couple*? And if so, why had her dad failed to mention it? It's not like Anne wanted her dad to be alone for the rest of his life or anything; she just wasn't sure she was ready for him to start dating just yet. Especially since she'd just started spending time with him again, and she really didn't feel like sharing.

Thinking about her dad always made her think about her mom. And now she wondered if she wasn't turning out to be exactly like her—and not in a good way. Her mom had obsessed over some guy to the point where she'd jeopardized her entire family, and now Anne was sitting here doing the same kind of thing.

Here she was, sitting at an overdecorated table (what was with all the big golden candelabras?) at what most people would consider to be a great party (if for no other reason than the free booze and drunken B-list celebs), and she wasn't even enjoying it because she was too busy thinking about some guy who didn't even have the decency to show up. It was truly pathetic.

"Hey, you guys," she said, trying to get Lola's and Diego's attention. She was determined to have some fun. "You wanna walk around and eavesdrop on the stars or something?"

They both turned to look at her with forced patience. Then, simultaneously shaking their heads no, they immediately went back to their private conversation. *Fine, then. I'll have fun by myself,* Anne thought, grabbing her purse and getting up from the table.

Spying Duncan across the room, she made a beeline right for him. "What are you drinking?" she asked, peering at his tall glass filled with clear, bubbly liquid with a wedge of lime suspended in the middle.

"Club soda," he said, smiling sheepishly.

"It's an open bar, you know." She laughed, shaking her head.

"Yeah, but my dad will kill me if anything happens to his car, so I'm not taking any chances." He shrugged. "So where is everybody?"

"Well, I just left the two new lovebirds," Anne said, pointing at Lola and Diego.

"Yeah, what's up with that?" Duncan asked.

"Who knows?" Anne shrugged. "Also, I'm kind of avoiding my dad because I don't really want to know that he has a new girlfriend, even though it's obvious that he does. Not to mention I thought Chris would have been here by now, but apparently he's still at Ellie's," she said, sounding bitter even though she'd aimed for nonchalance.

"Chris is at Ellie's?" Duncan asked, eyes going wide.

"Yeah," Anne said, feeling suddenly really uncomfortable. "You didn't know?"

"Not exactly." He shook his head. "I invited her tonight and she said she wasn't feeling well and had to rest up, since the Surf Fest thing is in two weeks and her dad booked her a coach again for tomorrow. She didn't say anything about Chris being with her." He looked upset.

Great, thought Anne. *It's not enough that my love life sucks. Now I had to go and wreck Duncan's as well.* "Oh, well, Chris told me they were assigned as lab partners, and they were just starting a project and got a little behind. But he'd meet me here later," she said, shrugging as she looked toward the door. "I stopped holding my breath about an hour ago." She smiled.

"I should have known," Duncan said, shaking his head. "It's always been about Chris."

"What're you talking about?" Anne asked, fearing what he was about to say, yet still needing to hear it.

"Ellie's liked Chris forever. It's so obvious, but she thinks she's the only one who knows. That night when we hooked up at the beach, I really thought she was finally getting over him. I should have known she was just trying to get back at him."

"Get back at him for what?" Anne asked, confused.

"For liking you," he said, looking right at her and taking a sip of his drink.

chapter thirty-nine

"Do you think everyone's still here?" Ellie asked as Chris pulled up to the valet.

"Who knows?" He shrugged. "I guess we'll see when we get in there."

"Will they let us in?" she asked, running her fingers through her long blond hair that she was wearing down for a change. "I mean, don't we have to be on a list or something?"

"No worries," he said, getting out of the car and handing over his keys. "Anne said she put me on it, so I'm sure I can get you in, too." He smiled.

Yeah, only she probably put me on the do-not-let-in-under-any-circumstances list, thought Ellie, following right behind him. It had been pretty awful of her to take advantage of Chris's good nature by pretending to be so overstressed about school and Surf Fest and her dad and insisting on getting a head start on the science project. And even then, she'd made sure that it took way longer than necessary by pretending to not fully understand the concept, when, if anything, she'd understood it even better than he did. She rolled her eyes just thinking about it. That was definitely an all-new low for her—*dumbing it down for a guy.*

And now, as she walked into the party and scanned the room,

she was feeling pretty ashamed. *Well, at least Duncan won't be here, since I lied to him, too,* she thought.

Relieved that she hadn't spotted any of her friends, Ellie grabbed Chris's hand and pulled him toward the bar. "I really want a drink," she said, feeling suddenly pleased with herself when she saw the expression on his face. It was nice to be able to shock someone you'd known for years.

She grabbed a glass of champagne for each of them. Then, turning to hand him one, she was disappointed when he shook his head no. "Just water for me," he said. "It's late, I'm tired, and it's a long drive home."

"Fine. More for me," she said, holding up the two flutes and smiling, but then feeling kind of stupid immediately afterward.

"Glad you could make it," she heard someone say, the voice coming from right behind her.

She turned to see Duncan standing there staring at her. "Duncan, hey. Um, I thought you weren't gonna show," she said, sipping her champagne nervously and avoiding his eyes. *Oh great, this is my karma,* she thought. *And there's no doubt I deserve this.*

"Is that why *you* showed?" he asked, noticing the two drinks she was holding and giving her an odd look.

"What? No! Of course not, don't be silly," she said, laughing outwardly while feeling totally panicked inside. "Do you want some?" She offered the extra flute, but he shook his head no. "So, who'd you come with?" She took another hefty sip, hoping it would calm her nerves, and get her through this.

"I drove up with Lola, but I've been hanging with Anne," he said, nodding toward the table where Anne was sitting.

"Oh." Ellie glanced quickly at Anne, feeling a stab of guilt at seeing her sitting alone.

"So where'd Chris go?" Duncan asked, looking around.

Ellie shrugged, hoping Duncan couldn't tell how nervous she was. "Duncan, I—" She faltered, and started again. "I know how this looks. But the truth is, we were working on a project, for school, and it was so intense that we just decided to drive up here and blow off a little steam. I was totally going to call you, but then I realized how late it was." She shrugged, fully aware of how lame she sounded. There was no way he was buying her lousy excuses.

He just stood there looking at her, not saying anything.

"Hey." Chris walked up. "I just saw Anne sitting over there by herself. Why don't we go join her?" he said, already turning and motioning for them to follow.

Of course, Ellie thought, as she watched him walk away. *It's always gonna be about Anne. And I've been a total fool to think otherwise.*

chapter forty

Diego is so amazing, Lola thought, smiling as he told yet another hilarious story. Who would have thought her mom would actually introduce her to someone she had so much in common with? They loved the same movies, the same books, the same magazines, the same music, the same television shows, the same celebrities, the same clothing designers—they even liked the same hair products! But more important, they both knew firsthand what it was like to grow up with strict, overbearing parents who had even stricter ideas on how their children should and would live their lives.

It's like we're soul mates, she thought, looking into his gorgeous, dark, and long-lashed eyes. *Soul mates who would never, ever sleep together.*

"I can't wait 'til next fall," he said, taking a sip of red wine.

"Why? What's happening next fall?" she asked.

"I'll be going to Columbia, living in my own apartment three thousand miles away from my parents' watchful eyes. Free at last in New York City! It doesn't get any better than that." He smiled.

"Sounds great," Lola agreed.

"Yeah." He nodded. "All I have to do now is lay low, stay under their radar, and just get through my last year of high school," he said.

Lola looked at him. He was gorgeous, smart, ambitious, funny, totally presentable, and he'd already won the approval of her parents. In other words, *he was perfect.*

"I have an idea," she said, smiling and leaning toward him.

chapter forty-one

Ellie looked at Duncan standing in front of her. He was sweet, nice, cute, funny, athletic—so why couldn't she like him? *There must be something wrong with me,* she thought.

"I think I'm gonna take off," he said, looking at her and shrugging. "Can you tell Lola and make sure she has a ride home?"

"Oh. Okay. Sure." Ellie felt awful about lying to him, and even worse about having been caught. *He has no idea how lucky he is that I don't like him,* she thought. *Because he definitely deserves someone much nicer than me.* "But Duncan, um, you don't have to go," she said, wondering if she really did want him to stay or if she was just trying to alleviate her own guilt. *Probably the latter.*

"No, I should hit it. I'm surfing in a contest tomorrow and I've got a seven-thirty heat." he told her.

"Oh, okay, well, good luck," she said, standing there with her two champagne glasses, one empty, the other completely full.

As she watched him fumble with his keys, she contemplated asking him for a ride. She too needed to get some sleep if she was going to be in a halfway decent form for Lina tomorrow. But it was pretty obvious he just wanted to get away from her, so she just stood there and watched him walk out the door, wondering how she was going to get home. *It's not like I can ask Chris,* she thought, glancing over to see him leaning close to Anne, talking intently, his arm around her shoulder.

"Just FYI, don't be fooled by the Colin Farrell lookalike over there," Jade said, walking up and pointing toward a table in the far corner of the room.

"Colin Farrell? Are you serious?" Ellie asked, all excited. Not that she was a big fan of his, but she'd yet to see one big name and she'd been here at least twenty minutes.

"No, I repeat, *not Colin*. He has the hair, the tats, the sexy smirk, but up close, I'm telling ya, it's just fool's gold," Jade said, crossing her arms and shaking her head. "*Extremely* disappointing. Anyway, have you had any Ben sightings? Know where he might be?"

"I thought he was with you." Ellie shrugged and set both champagne glasses on the edge of a nearby table.

"He was, but then I saw the Colin wannabe and made a mad dash across the room so I could get a closer look. You know how I love my bad boys." She laughed.

"And now you can't locate the one you came with," Ellie said, smiling.

"Jeez, I hope he hasn't had any more to drink," Jade said, scanning the room with a worried look on her face. "Last time I saw him, he wasn't looking so great."

"Does he have a problem?" Ellie asked, already assuming the answer.

"Actually, he has a lot of problems," Jade said. "But he's going through a really rough time right now, so it's totally understandable. He's a really great person though, and I know he's gonna pull through this. It's just a matter of time." She nodded.

Ellie watched Jade's eyes search the room, looking for Ben. He may be a nice guy, like Jade had said, but she doubted he'd pull out of it anytime soon. She recognized a downward spiral when she saw one. But it's not like she could tell Jade that. Jade would just get mad and accuse her of being judgmental. *Besides, with the way I've been handling my own life lately, I really don't have the right to judge anyone else,* she thought.

"Oh, maybe this is him," Jade said, grabbing her ringing cell phone and placing her free hand over her other ear. "What happened? . . . Oh, great. Just stay right there." She closed her phone and looked at Ellie. "Ben got kicked out and they won't let him back in."

"Why?" Ellie asked, wondering what he could have possibly done to get kicked out of a party like this, where all the normal rules of behavior had seemingly been abandoned.

"I have no idea, but clearly the party's over for me. I gotta drive him home," she said, shaking her head and rifling through her purse for her car keys.

Ellie looked over at Chris and Anne. It was like they were in their own little world. And while she really didn't want to ride home with Ben, she was pretty much out of options. "Do you have room for one more?" she asked.

chapter forty-two

Anne looked toward the door just in time to see Ellie leave. She was embarrassed to think how ridiculous she'd been, worrying about them studying together. Chris was acting so sweet and affectionate, holding her hand and smiling, and even though it wasn't turning out anything like the movie version she'd scripted in her head, it was still pretty nice, maybe even better. Because this was real. "I'm so glad you made it here," she said, leaning toward him and smiling.

"Sorry it wasn't sooner, but Ellie was really freaked out about the project. She gets so stressed sometimes." He shook his head.

"Hmm." Anne smiled politely. The last thing she wanted to do was talk about Ellie.

"And she just couldn't seem to grasp the concept," he continued. "Which is *so weird,* because normally she's a whiz at science. But we had to go over it again and again, until finally I just asked her if we could put it away, 'cause I had to meet you. But then she got all stressed again, so I just decided to invite her." He shrugged. "I thought she needed to blow off a little steam, you know?"

Anne just looked at Chris and nodded. She knew he was telling the truth. But she also knew he was completely clueless to the fact that he'd just been totally played. *Guys so don't get girls,* she thought. But it's not like it mattered. He was with her now, and it was obvious that Ellie's sad little game had failed miserably. "Well, now that you're here, there's something I have to ask you," she said, smiling and leaning toward him.

"Anything." He grabbed both her hands.

"Do you wanna bail soon? This party isn't really as great as I thought it would be." She shrugged.

"Candelabras, an open bar, all the gourmet food you can eat, great music, table-dancing celebrities—and this party isn't fun enough for you?" he said, in mock surprise. "Just what kind of high-maintenance parties are you used to?"

"Honestly, I'm not really a party person," she admitted. "I'm really more the quiet type."

"Wanna go someplace quiet?" He smiled.

chapter forty-three

Ben was outside, sitting on the hood of Jade's car and looking pretty messed up. His blue eyes were bloodshot and etched with dark circles, his brown hair was all matted and tangled, and the sleeve of his striped shirt was ripped. "So what happened?" Jade asked, unlocking the door and motioning for him to get in the back.

"Some asshole kicked me out," he said, shaking his head and lunging onto the backseat.

"Well, what did you do?" Ellie asked, turning to look at him.

"Nothing. I didn't do anything, okay? That party's just full of pretentious Hollywood assholes," he said, looking at her.

"Well, you must have done something," Ellie insisted, not believing his version for one second and not willing to let it go, either.

"Whatever." He glared at her from the backseat. "Think what you want. But I was just minding my own business."

"Okay, you guys. Everybody just relax, okay?" Jade pleaded, merging onto the freeway and turning up her stereo. "Let's just chill out and listen to some tunes. We'll be home before you know it."

"Whatever," Ben said from the backseat, rolling his eyes.

"Fine with me," Ellie said, folding her arms across her chest and staring out the window. She couldn't wait to get home and into her nice, warm bed. She leaned her head against the window and closed her eyes, wondering if this was her punishment for the whole Duncan mess. Because ending up spending an hour in the same car as Ben, who was not only snoring way louder than the music, but who totally reeked of alcohol and cigarettes, really did seem like bad karma. *Please, just get me home soon,* she thought, right before drifting off to sleep.

"Ellie! Hey, wake up." Jade tapped her hard on the shoulder.

"What? Are we home?" Ellie asked, rubbing her eyes and squinting at Jade.

"Almost, we're on Newport Coast, but this cop has been following us for like a mile now, and I'm starting to get a little freaked."

Ellie turned in her seat and saw the police car following closely behind them. "Were you speeding?" she asked.

"No. Speed limit the whole way, I swear. I don't know what his problem is," she said, glancing nervously at the rearview mirror.

"You know, I read recently that when a cop wants to find a drunk driver, they look for the guy who's driving *too perfect,*" Ellie told her.

"So what are you suggesting? That I start driving all erratic, so he'll move on to someone else?" She rolled her eyes. "Besides, I'm not drunk. I haven't had anything to drink all night."

"Don't worry about it, then. I'm sure it's nothing," Ellie said, just about to close her eyes again when the squad car pulled up next to them with siren wailing and lights flashing.

chapter forty-four

"Where are you taking me?" Anne asked, struggling to keep up with Chris as he pulled her through the crowd of people. "You act like you know your way around this place or something," she said.

"Never been here before in my life." He looked back at her and smiled. "But I have been in a few restaurants, and I happen to know that the one thing they all have in common, besides food, is a back door. See, I told you!" he said, opening the door and leading her through it.

They entered into a beautiful lush courtyard lit by glowing white candles and filled with tall flowering trees, colorful hanging plants, and a beautiful mosaic fountain built right in the middle of it all.

"Wow, this is beautiful. I wonder why nobody's out here?" Anne said, looking at the empty linen-covered tables and rod iron chairs.

"Maybe 'cause there's no bar," Chris said, putting his arms around her and pulling her toward him.

His face was so close to hers she could feel his soft breath on her cheek, and just as he was about to kiss her, she whispered,

"Shh! Did you hear that?" Her eyes went wide as she looked around cautiously.

"I didn't hear anything," Chris mumbled, eyes still closed while he nuzzled her neck. "You're imagining things."

"I'm serious," she insisted. "Someone's out here. Listen!"

Chris reluctantly pulled away and quickly looked around. "Relax; it's just us," he said, leaning toward her again, determined to kiss her this time.

"I know I heard something," she said, sounding completely paranoid.

"So what?" Chris shrugged, kissing the side of her neck since she wouldn't stop talking. "It's probably just Brad and Jen, avoiding the paparazzi and getting a little fresh air."

Anne looked at him and laughed. "Brad and Jen? They are *so over*." She shook her head. "You are so out of touch!" she said, finally leaning in to kiss him.

His hands were wrapped tightly around her waist, while hers were tangled in his soft, shaggy hair when someone walked up behind them and said, "Anne? Is that you?"

Oh God, oh no, don't let it be . . . , she thought, pulling away from Chris and wiping her mouth with the back of her hand. Then, slowly looking up, she saw her dad and Brooke standing there, his lips holding traces of Brooke's frosty peach lipstick.

Oh sick, they both came out here for the same reason! Which meant she'd been making out just steps away from her dad! It didn't get any grosser than that.

"Um, Chris and I were just talking," she said, immediately realizing how totally lame it sounded. "I mean, we were just getting some air . . . because . . . you know . . . it's so *stuffy* in there." She pointed toward the restaurant. *Oh yeah, that was convincing,* she thought, glancing briefly at Chris, who looked as embarrassed as she felt.

"Well, now that you've gotten some air, what do you say we all go back inside?" her dad said, giving them a stern parental look.

Oh please, like you're any better, Anne thought. *You're the parent! You're the one who should be setting the example!*

But she didn't say that. Instead she just gave him a sheepish look and said, "Um, okay."

chapter forty-five

"Oh, great," Jade said, shaking her head as she pulled over to the side of the road and came to a complete stop.

"What do you think he wants?" Ellie asked nervously.

"Well, I think we're about to find out." Jade rolled down her window and smiled politely. "Hi, officer. Is something wrong?" she asked.

"Did you know that your left taillight is out?" he said, pointing his flashlight into the car, going from Jade to Ellie, then focusing on Ben, who was sprawled out in the back, sound asleep, and not wearing a seat belt.

"Oh, really? Um, no, I had no idea," Jade said, cautiously.

"Can I see your license and registration, please?"

Jade reached for her wallet with hands that were shaking so bad she could barely open it. "Here," she said, handing over her license while Ellie searched through the mess of papers in the glove compartment, looking for the registration.

Tomorrow I will clean out this car. Tomorrow I will fix my taillight. Tomorrow I will organize my life. I really hope I make it to tomorrow, Jade thought.

"Who's been drinking?" the cop asked, watching Jade closely as he handed the papers to his partner.

"Um, they have," Jade said, pointing at Ellie and Ben. "I was just making sure everyone got home safely."

The cop stood there, eyes narrowed, looking at all three of them. "I'd like you to step out of the car, please."

"What? But why?" Jade asked, totally panicked now. No good could come of this.

"Just step out of the car," he said. "All of you."

chapter forty-six

"Do you really have to call *all* of our parents?" Jade asked, glancing nervously at Ellie, whose face had gone completely white and who looked like she was about to pass out at any second. She was way more worried about Ellie than herself, especially if they called Ellie's dad.

They were sitting in a small room at the Newport Beach police station, where they'd been for the last half hour—ever since Ben had failed the Breathalyzer test and they found the Baggie full of pot he'd thrown on the floor of the car. At first, Jade was being held responsible for the pot—her car, her possession, they'd reasoned. But since she'd breathed clean, while Ben was obviously drunk and stoned, and since the bag was found on the floor right next to his feet, they decided to let her off with just a minor curfew violation, while Ben was in another room being processed for possession and underage drinking.

The only crime poor Ellie committed was being in the wrong place at the wrong time, Jade thought, looking at her friend and feeling really guilty for getting her into this mess.

"I mean, I was the driver, so if you have to call my parents, then fine. But Ellie just needed a ride. I swear, she didn't do anything wrong. So can you maybe just like, let her go?" Jade pleaded.

"Sorry. Your parents have already been notified. They'll be here any minute," the cop said, leaving them alone in the room to wait out their fate.

Ellie looked at Jade, her eyes welling up with tears. "Well, it's been nice knowing ya," she said, looking nervously toward the door.

"Oh God, El, I am *so sorry*. I don't know what else to say." Jade hugged her. Even though technically it was totally Ben's fault, Jade took full responsibility where Ellie was concerned. But what made it even worse was knowing how Ellie felt about Ben, and how she'd tried to warn her.

Jade also thought it was weird how Ben was always ragging on his dad, and yet he'd been the one to come bail him out. And even though Jade had only gotten a quick glimpse of him, he really didn't look so awful. He just looked really worried.

"That's it. I'm dead," Ellie whispered, seeing her dad enter the room.

"Ellie, honey, are you okay?" he asked, swooping her into his arms and hugging her so tight she could barely catch her breath.

"Yeah. I'm fine, really. It wasn't that big of a deal," she said, raising her eyebrows at Jade as her dad continued to hug her, refusing to let her go. "It was just an overinflated fix-it ticket." She laughed, obviously relieved that he wasn't reacting in the way she'd expected.

"Let's get you home." He put his arm around her protectively and walked her to the door. Then, turning to look at Jade, he said, "I just spoke to your parents. They're on their way."

Jade watched Ellie and her dad leave, feeling totally relieved that he hadn't been nearly as angry and upset as she had assumed he'd be. And if *he* was acting that cool and casual about it, then surely her own parents would be a total breeze.

"Hey!" Jade said, seeing them standing in the doorway. She

smiled and jumped up from her chair, in anticipation of a big group hug.

"Grab your belongings," her father said sternly, while her mother stood silently, with her arms folded across her chest. "We'll talk when we get home."

chapter forty-seven

With Surf Fest now just three days away, it was taking all of Ellie's concentration not to be distracted by everyone around her. First, there was Duncan's insistence on ignoring her. Not that she expected anything different, and *not* that she even really cared, but still, she'd really hoped they could just move on and go right back to their old, platonic ways. But apparently Duncan had other ideas. Because not only had he stopped calling, but now he barely spoke to her at school, despite the fact that they shared two classes and sat at the same lunch table. She was surprised that she was so bothered by it—but it was probably only because she couldn't stand to hurt anyone's feelings.

And then there were Chris and Anne. The perfect, happy couple, who seemed to be everywhere Ellie was. Seriously, there was no safe place. They shared the same neighborhood, the same school, the same lunch table, the same friends, the same gym, and, worst of all, even the same waves. There was just no avoiding them, so Ellie had simply stopped trying. She was learning to ignore them just like Duncan ignored her.

And ever since the party, Lola and Diego were rarely apart. The only time Ellie got to see her now was at school, and Ellie was certain that was only because Diego was enrolled elsewhere. But even at school it was always Diego this and Diego that. It kind of bugged Ellie when girls did things like that—got all impressed over every little thing their boyfriend did. But still, it was pretty great to see Lola so happy and in love—even if Diego was kind of a strange choice.

And then there was Jade, who was under severe house arrest and was only allowed to go to school and then straight home again. Who would have thought that Ellie's dad would be so understanding and forgiving, while Jade's parents would totally lay down the law?

Even Ellie's brother, Dean, had been acting really bizarre lately, not going out with his friends, barely surfing. He just sat in his room, staring at his computer for hours on end, almost like he was stuck in his own, self-inflicted house arrest.

But unfortunately, her dad was right back to his normal, domineering self. The emotional generosity he'd shown at the police station had lasted only until the next morning. Then it was back to the usual pep talks, lectures, and dire warnings.

Ellie zipped up the back of her wetsuit, grabbed her board, and headed down the beach stairs toward the ocean. Dropping her board in the water, she paddled out, determined to clear her mind of everything but her surfboard and the waves. The competition came first right now, and everything else would just have to wait.

chapter forty-eight

Lola was lying on her bed, with the phone to her ear, talking to Diego and laughing hysterically—until her mom barged in without knocking.

"I gotta go. I'll call you later," she told him, tossing her phone onto her nightstand and giving her mother an annoyed look. "Excuse me, but could you please knock next time? Is that too much to ask?" she said, shaking her head and rolling her eyes. She'd been getting away with all kinds of rude behavior lately—ever since Diego came into her life. It's like her mom was so elated at her obvious matchmaking success that she was letting all the usual infractions slip past without mention.

"In case you've forgotten, we need to be at the dressmaker's in fifteen minutes." Her mother gazed into Lola's mirror and adjusted her blazer.

"What for?" Lola asked, rifling through some books on her shelf, searching for the one she promised to lend Diego.

"Today is your final fitting. Cotillion is this weekend! Or have you forgotten that, too?" She turned to look at her daughter.

Oh God, the dreaded cotillion. All the etiquette classes, all the waltzing, all the sweaty-palmed geeks insisting on leading when she knew the dance better than they did—it all culminated in this one big, overblown moment that she wanted nothing to do with. She had no interest in showing off her newly acquired curtsey, her fancy manners, her slick dance moves, or her dad's hefty bank account. Not to mention that hideous poufy white dress she was supposed to wear.

"Mom, I really don't feel up to it today," she said.

"Don't say another word. You are going and that's final. *Abuela* is already in the car, waiting. She's waited her whole life for this moment and you will not disappoint her."

Poor Abuela, *that can't be true,* Lola thought, hoping her mom was exaggerating as usual.

"Now, put on some shoes and let's go," her mother said as she walked out the door.

Fine, Lola thought. *I'll play along today, but Saturday is another story.*

chapter forty-nine

If I have to spend one more second inside this house, I'm going to burst, thought Jade. She'd always liked school, though she definitely liked it most when the final bell rang. But now that her parents had put her under strict house arrest, the hours between eight and three had suddenly become a lot more meaningful. It was the only time she had for any social interaction, not to mention *freedom*. And the really sad, sick thing was that now she actually found herself *dreading* the sound of the final bell.

The only good thing (and she'd searched high and low to find one) was that she now had complete possession of the remote control between the hours of three and six, when nobody else was home. But unfortunately she'd also discovered that it was only worth having the remote when someone else wanted it.

Getting up from the couch, she walked over to the big bay window, pressing her forehead against the glass and staring with longing at the distant ocean view, wondering if this meant the end of her competing in Surf Fest. She'd competed every year since she first learned to surf, and even though she didn't take it as seriously as Ellie, she still looked forward to the event all year. But even though her parents had gone totally overboard with her punishment, she was positive that if she just kept to her best be-havior, and observed all the rules, then she'd ultimately be awarded a reduced sentence and get to compete on Saturday.

She thought about Ben, wondering how he was doing. His mom had called a few days ago to apologize for everything and tell her he was living with his dad now. Jade was glad he was try-ing to work things out, but more than a little annoyed that he hadn't bothered to call himself. After all, she'd gone out of her way to help him, had done everything she could to be there for him. Still, lately she'd begun to realize that he hadn't exactly asked for her support. And, just maybe, he had never actually wanted it.

chapter fifty

Anne was really nervous about mentioning Surf Fest to her dad—partly because she was nervous about it in general, and partly because she was afraid he wouldn't show. Yet she was also equally worried that he *would* show. Because then he might bring Brooke. And Brooke was a subject that neither one of them seemed very willing to talk about.

Ever since they'd caught each other making out at the party, they seemed to adopt this silent agreement to never, ever mention it again. Which was fine by Anne. Just thinking about it still totally grossed her out.

The only one who knew about her surfing, other than her friends at school, was Jake. And there was no way he'd tell, as Anne had blackmailed, bribed, and basically sworn him to secrecy.

A few days ago she'd been in the home office printing all the contest info, when he walked in.

"You're competing in Surf Fest?" he'd asked, peering over her shoulder, eyes wide with surprise.

"Maybe. I haven't actually decided yet, so don't say anything to anybody. Especially my dad," she'd said, turning to look at him.

"Why not? He'll be totally stoked."

"Jake, I'm serious. If you so much as tell him, then I'll . . ." She hesitated, trying to think of something good. "I'll tell him you drink beer with your bros on our terrace." She narrowed her eyes at him.

"Dude, what's with the threats? You need to relax, okay? I'm not gonna say anything." He looked at her and shook his head. "But FYI, your dad's pretty Hollywood. I'm sure he's seen a lot worse than a couple of guys drinking a beer."

Anne just looked at him, not saying anything. Unfortunately, he was right. Her dad definitely led a way cooler life and went to way better parties than she did.

But now, with the event just days away, she really had to focus. And knowing she was nowhere near good enough to impress any of the judges, her only goals were to have some fun, learn the ropes, and hopefully not make a total fool of herself.

Going into her room, she got down on her hands and knees and slid her Indo Board out from under her bed. She was just about to hop on when her phone rang.

"Hello?" she said hurriedly. She was in no mood for conversation.

"Anne? How are you, honey?"

Oh, great. It was her mom again. She'd been leaving lots of messages in the past few days, but Anne hadn't gotten around to returning any of them. She'd been too busy with school, surfing, and Chris to even bother. Besides, the last thing she needed right now was another fight with her mom. "Oh, hey," she said, getting herself balanced on her board and positioning down into a low squat.

"I've been trying to reach you for days," her mother said.

"Yeah, I know. I'm sorry I haven't called; I've just been super busy with school and stuff," Anne said, walking slowly to the end of the board, while attempting to keep it perfectly balanced.

"Well, I was really wishing we could have talked sooner, because now you won't have much time to prepare."

"Prepare for what?" Anne asked, carefully studying her reflection in the full-length mirror.

"I've reserved you a ticket on the nonstop to New York this weekend."

"What?" Anne struggled to maintain her balance.

"Your flight leaves Friday at twelve thirty your time, and lands in New York around nine fifteen our time. I've arranged for a limo to pick you up and bring you straight to the Four Seasons. That's where we'll all be staying."

"What are you talking about?" Anne asked, standing very still, while the muscles in her legs worked overtime, trying to keep her from tipping over.

"I'm getting married. And I want you to be my maid of honor."

"Mom. Oh my God. You can't be serious." Anne gripped the phone so tightly, her knuckles were fading. "I mean, are you and Dad even divorced yet?"

"The divorce has been final for weeks," her mother said, in the clipped voice she usually reserved for the courtroom.

"Weeks? You've been divorced for just a few weeks? And you think that's a sufficient amount of time to just jump back in and do it all over again?" Anne waited for a response, but all she got was the sound of light breathing. "It's like, did it ever occur to you to run it by *me* first? I am still your daughter, right? I mean, how could you do this? I've only met him once!"

"Twice, Anne. You've met him twice."

"Whatever! Twice. Fine. Do I get *any* say in this?" she asked, starting to feel really nauseous and fighting to keep her balance.

"I'm sorry, Anne, but no. I'm the adult. It's my decision. And it's already been booked and paid for. All I request from you is your presence as my maid of honor," she said.

Maid of honor? More like maid of horror! There's no way she's guilt-

ing me into this, Anne thought. *And if she thinks she's acting like an adult, well, then she's totally delusional.* "I'm sorry, but I can't make it," Anne said, watching herself in the mirror as she broke her mother's heart.

"Why not?"

"Well, for starters Friday is a school day, in case you've forgotten. And I can't go missing a whole day of school just because you started feeling all romantic and decided to pull a Britney Spears. And second, for your information I've made a life for myself here. I have friends, I have plans for this weekend, and I just can't put everything on hold because of your whims."

"It's hardly a whim, Anne," her mother said, blowing loudly into a tissue.

"Oh, that's right; I forgot. You two have been having a relationship for *years* now."

"Anne, I don't have time for this. So just tell me, are you coming or not?"

"I just don't get what the rush is. I mean, you're not pregnant, are you?" Anne laughed. The thought of her mother being pregnant was ridiculous. She was *old*. She was like, *over forty,* for God's sake. But when she stopped laughing, she realized the line had gone silent. *Oh God. Oh no. Please don't let it be true!* "Mom?" she whispered. "Is it true?"

"Is what true?" She sounded sad and very, very tired.

"What I just asked. Are you?" Anne couldn't finish the sentence. Now that it might be true, she couldn't bear to say the word out loud.

"I wasn't going to tell you until you got here," her mother said quietly.

"Oh." Anne's eyes started to sting as she fought back the tears. "Well, I wish you all the best. But I just can't support this. I'm sorry, but I just . . ." She stopped and wiped her hand across her eyes. "I just can't. And I've already got plans this weekend. I'm doing something that means a lot to me. Something that you know nothing about. But I guess there's a lot we don't know about each other these days," she said, swallowing hard.

"If you change your mind, there will be a ticket on hold for you at the Delta ticket counter," her mother told her, suddenly sounding all businesslike and professional again.

"I'm sorry, but that's not gonna happen," Anne said, flipping her phone closed, and allowing herself to fall straight off the Indo Board and right onto her ass.

chapter fifty-one

"What about that one?" Lola asked.

"Definitely gay." Diego nodded.

"No! Don't say that! He's *so* cute! Besides, you've said that about the last four guys I've picked."

"That's because the last four *were* gay." He smiled.

"Then I dare you to find me one that isn't," she said, narrowing her eyes at him.

"Okay. How about that guy right over there." Diego pointed.

"The one in the Hooters T-shirt, with the mullet and the beer gut? *Is that the one?* Gee, thanks a lot." Lola laughed and punched him in the arm. They had somehow survived the last of the many cotillion rehearsals and now they were lounging on one of the benches on Main Beach, eating frozen yogurt and watching all the people. "I double-dare you to find me another one," she said. "And this time, make sure he's cute."

Diego removed his sunglasses and scanned the beach. In the last week they had known each other they'd become extremely close, confiding all their dreams and secrets through late-night telephone calls and early-morning IMs. They had also managed to successfully fool everyone they knew into believing that they were seriously dating. And it was going so smoothly, they figured they could carry on like this for years. Allowing them both to discreetly date the men of their choice while staying under their parents' hypersensitive radar. *It's genius,* Lola thought, *a definite no-brainer, and everybody wins.* The only thing she felt really bad about was lying to her friends. But if the plan was going to work, then no one could know the truth. Because the more people were in on it, the more potential there was for a major leak.

"Come on, Diego. There must be one gorgeous straight guy on this beach. Just one. That's all I ask. Lie to me if you have to," she pleaded.

"Hold on. Just give me a minute," he said, glancing at her briefly before getting back to the task at hand. "Oh. My. Wow. Lola, right in front of us. Twelve o'clock position. He's holding a surfboard and coming out of the ocean. And check out those abs!"

But Lola wasn't looking at his abs. Her eyes were fixated on his face. While her body felt sweaty, stiff, and solid like a block of ice.

"He's looking right at you, too! You little vixen!" He punched her playfully in the arm. "Wait. Is he? It seems like he's approaching us. Lola, do you know that guy?" he whispered, looking at her in shock.

Lola did know him. She knew him better than she'd ever known any guy. And she'd told him things she'd never told anyone else. Hell, up until a few weeks ago she even thought she loved him. But she couldn't tell Diego that. Because her mouth had suddenly grown so dry and parched, she wasn't even sure if she could speak. And now he was standing right in front of her.

"Hey," he said, running his hand through his wet, sandy hair and looking from Lola to Diego, and then back again.

"Hey," she said softly, forcing her lips into a half smile.

"So, how've you been?" he asked, looking right at her.

"Great!" she said, feigning an enthusiasm she definitely didn't feel. "How've you been?" She didn't want to be mean, but she was really hoping he hadn't been doing so great. She also hoped there were no yogurt chips stuck between her teeth.

"Okay." He shrugged.

"So how's the project coming along?" she asked.

"A little stalled, but . . ." He shrugged without finishing his sentence, but Lola was in no mood to finish it for him. Not anymore.

"Um, Lola," Diego said, giving her an impatient look while not so gently elbowing her in the ribs.

"Oh, I'm sorry. I totally forgot to introduce you guys. Diego, this is my ex-boyfriend and Ellie's brother, Dean." She pointed to the gorgeous surfer standing in front of them. "And Dean, this is my new boyfriend, Diego," she said, smiling brightly and leaning over to kiss Diego on the cheek.

chapter fifty-two

All day at school Ellie could barely concentrate. She had a major bad case of precompetition jitters. It was all she could think about. So when the final bell finally rang at exactly 3:20 P.M., she already had her car keys in hand and, for the first time ever, she was actually the first person out the door.

And she'd almost made it to the parking lot when she ran smack into Chris and Anne.

"Whoa, where you going in such a hurry?" he asked, leaning down to help her pick up all the books she'd dropped.

"Oh, I'm just trying to get home. I've got some stuff to do before registration tonight," she said, brushing some dirt off her AP History textbook and looking from Chris to Anne.

"We're headed up there later," he said, wrapping his arm casually around Anne's shoulders. "Why don't you ride with us?"

Ellie and Anne looked at each other, both obviously hating that idea. *Chris still doesn't get it,* Ellie thought, shaking her head and feeling totally annoyed with him. "That's okay, but thanks anyway," she said. Then looking right at Anne, she continued, "I'm surprised you're still competing. I mean, I would've thought you'd change your mind by now."

"What's that supposed to mean?" Anne asked, her eyes narrowing to angry slits.

"Well, we're the same age, so you'll be competing against *me*. I've been surfing for years and you're just starting out. I mean, I'd hate to see you embarrass yourself out there." Ellie looked right at her.

Anne just stood there, glaring at Ellie. "From what I've heard, it's just a really fun, laid-back event that's not all about winning and killer instinct. So I should be fine. It's *you* that should be worried," she said.

They both stood there, eyes narrowed, totally glaring at each other, while Chris looked increasingly uncomfortable. "Okay, that's enough. We're out of here," he said, pulling Anne away from Ellie and toward the parking lot. "See you tonight, El."

"Whatever," she said quietly, rolling her eyes as she watched them walk away, arm in arm.

chapter fifty-three

"God, she is such a bitch!" Anne said, shaking her head and looking out the window as Chris pulled out of the student lot. "I'm *so over* trying to be nice to her. You heard her this time. So even you can't deny it anymore."

"Okay, so she was a little harsh," he said, turning to look at her briefly. "She just gets really wound up, you know? But really, she's not as bad as you think. I mean, maybe you should just cut her some slack."

"You've got to be kidding? I mean, why would I do that? You heard the same thing I just did!" Anne said, feeling totally frustrated with his refusal to see Ellie for what she really was—a conniving, nasty control freak. She shook her head and stared at him.

"Listen, you haven't known her as long as I have. She's been through a really rough time the last couple years."

"For your information, I'm going through a rough time, too. But you don't see *me* treating people like that."

"What are you talking about?" he asked, glancing at her briefly before turning left on PCH.

"Nothing, forget it," she said, crossing her arms in front of her and looking out the window. She was dying to confide in someone about her mom, but this was definitely not the right time. Not to mention that it was beginning to seem like he might not be the right person.

"All right, so she got a little bitchy with you. Why can't you just let it go? I mean, what's the big deal?"

Anne turned to face him. Was he serious? And why should she let it go? She'd put up with it long enough as it was. "I guess the big deal is that you always seem to be sticking up for *her* instead of *me*."

"That's not true," he said, shaking his head. "Look, I've known her for a really long time, and I guess I just don't see her the same way you do, that's all."

"Well, I guess it's easy for you to say that, since she'd never treat *you* like that. She's totally in love with you!" Anne said, still glaring at him.

"What? Are you serious?" He looked at her.

"You didn't know?" Anne asked, regretting having told him as soon as she saw the look on his face. Was he surprised? Was he flattered? She really couldn't tell, but whatever he felt, she knew it wasn't good. She watched him avoid her eyes now, staring straight ahead at the road in front of them, his hands gripping the wheel in the proper ten and two position, instead of his usual left hand on six, right hand on hers.

And by the time he pulled up to the Laguna Cove security gate they still hadn't said a single word to each other, and Anne wasn't sure how to break the silence.

How had things gotten so awkward so quickly? Had he really not realized how Ellie felt about him? And now that he did know, had he decided that he liked her, too?

Chris pulled up to her driveway and slowed to a stop. Normally he would park the car, get out, and come inside for a little while. But now he just sat there with the engine idling.

"So what time are you picking me up?" she asked, watching his face like a detective, searching for clues as to what could possibly be going on in his head.

"I don't know. What time's registration?" he asked, rubbing his chin and looking at her, but only briefly.

"I'm not sure, exactly. But I was thinking we could get there around seven and it should be fine. There's supposed to be live music and food and stuff," she said, her voice trailing off, noticing how distracted he seemed.

"Yeah, I know. I've been a few times," he told her.

"Okay, well, you wanna come in?" she asked, opening the car door and grabbing her purse.

He shook his head. "I can't. Listen, I don't know what time I'll be by so I'll just call you a little later, okay?"

She stared at him for a moment. Did he really want to leave it like this? Because she just wasn't capable of that. "Uh, is something wrong?" she asked, reaching down to grab her books.

"No. Why?" he asked, attempting that famous smile of his. But it wasn't really working this time.

"Never mind," she said, getting out of the car and closing the door between them. "I'll talk to you later."

Walking in the door, she saw Jake sitting at the kitchen table across from her dad and Brooke. *Oh great,* she thought, *just what I need, a nice, cozy family gathering.*

"Hey, honey, how was your day?" her dad asked, looking up from his pile of papers and smiling at her.

"Okay." She shrugged, setting down her books and grabbing a container of yogurt from the fridge and a spoon from the drawer.

"What are you doing?" she asked, going over to where they were working and leaning against the table.

"Just going over some numbers," her dad said, looking up at her briefly. "Hey, try not to spoil your appetite."

"Why?" she asked, enjoying another spoonful.

"We're all going out to dinner tonight, to celebrate."

"Celebrate what?" What could there possibly be to celebrate? Her mother and her shotgun marriage? Her boyfriend, who had just discovered he was in love with someone else? But her dad didn't know about any of those things, so it couldn't be that. Besides, he wasn't nearly as cynical and sarcastic as she was.

"We've been green-lighted for our next project. And some really big names have signed on," he said. "So I've booked us a table at Studio."

"What's that?" Anne asked, scraping the bottom of her yogurt cup with her spoon.

"Supposed to be one of the best restaurants in town," he told her.

"Well, maybe you can find someone to take my place. I kind of have plans." She looked briefly at Brooke, who, up until now, she'd been trying not to look at.

"So bring Chris. He's more than welcome." Her father smiled.

"Well, actually." She hesitated. "We're supposed to go to this party at San Onofre tonight."

"Can you skip it?" he asked.

"Not really. I'm kind of supposed to register for tomorrow," she told him.

"Are we talking in code?" her father asked, shaking his head. "Can you fill me in here? Register for what?"

"Well, I've decided to enter this surf contest." She studied his face closely, trying to determine whether or not Jake had betrayed her confidence.

"I didn't know you were that good." His eyes lit up as a proud smile spread across his face.

"Believe me, I'm not. I just really love surfing, and I kind of miss competing. And this is supposed to be really low-key and fun, so I figured it would be a good opportunity to get my feet wet. So to speak." She laughed. "I mean, I'll probably just totally embarrass myself, since I'm really not very good yet. But I gotta start somewhere, right?"

"When were you planning on telling me this?" he asked.

"Maybe never?" She shrugged. "I mean, you totally don't have to go. It'll probably be really embarrassing for you to watch me wipe out and stuff."

"Nonsense. We're definitely going," he said.

We? She looked over at Brooke, who was nodding and smiling. *Oh great, she's coming, too,* Anne thought. *So let's see, in the course of one weekend, I'm losing my boyfriend but gaining a new daddy, a new sibling, and possibly a new mommy. . . .*

It really didn't seem like a fair trade.

chapter fifty-four

Lola was sitting in the passenger seat of Ellie's Mini Cooper, singing along to the radio as they drove down the 5 freeway. The top was down, the cool wind was rushing against her cheeks, and her hair was loose and slapping lightly at the air around her head. She loved moments like this, when everything just felt so free and full of promise.

"So where's Diego tonight?" Ellie asked, glancing at her briefly as she merged into the exit lane.

Lola shrugged. "I think he's out with some friends, enjoying a boys' night out or something," she told her, laughing inside at the huge difference between what Ellie probably thought that meant and the reality.

"So are you guys, like, pretty serious, or what?" she asked, slowing as she exited the freeway

"I don't know." Lola shifted uncomfortably. She felt bad about lying to her friend, but she really had no choice, since she and Diego both agreed that absolutely no one could know the truth.

"Well, you're together all the time, and you seem really happy," Ellie pressed, refusing to let it go.

Lola sighed. "Well, he is pretty awesome. And yeah, we have been spending a lot of time together, but mostly it's because of the cotillion. It'll probably slow down a bit once we're past all that. I mean, it's better if we take it slow, you know?" she said, noticing a total hottie in the parking lot and suddenly realizing how awkward it would be to flirt with him now that everyone thought she was committed. *Hmmm, maybe we should have thought this through a little better,* she thought. *Maybe if I just tell Ellie, and swear her to secrecy . . .*

"Dean said he saw you guys at the beach," Ellie said, killing the engine and pulling her key from the ignition.

"Oh, really?" Lola flipped down the mirrored visor and checked out her lip gloss.

"Yeah, he said you guys looked really cozy together." Ellie was looking right at her.

"Hmmm," Lola muttered, casually flipping the mirror back up and opening her door. *Maybe I won't tell Ellie just yet. Maybe I'll keep it a secret just a little bit longer.*

chapter fifty-five

Just as Anne was getting out of the shower, she heard her phone beeping. Wrapping one towel around her head like a turban and another tightly around her body, she walked over to her desk, flipped open her phone, and listened to the message.

"Hey Anne, it's me, Chris. Um, sorry [static] but I'm not gonna be [static] but I'm still gonna try [static] okay [more static and then nothing]."

After replaying it three times, trying to hear through all the static, she finally just erased it and threw her phone on the bed. Bad reception or not, she knew when she was getting dumped. And that brief message had exhibited all the signs.

She finished drying off, dragged a comb through her wet, tangled hair, and then stood in front of the mirror staring at her reflection. *I have no idea what just happened,* she thought, *but there's no way I'm calling him back to find out.*

Then she threw on her robe and padded down the hall to where her father was still sitting at the kitchen table.

"Hey, Dad?" she said, standing next to him and dripping water onto the floor.

"Yeah?" He and Brooke both looked at her.

"I just have to make one quick stop before I meet you at the restaurant, okay?" she said, turning and heading back to her room before he even had a chance to answer.

chapter fifty-six

"It's so weird, not having Jade here," Ellie said. She'd already registered for tomorrow's first heat, and now they were sitting on a blanket on the sand, eating fish tacos and listening to the all-girl band.

"I know." Lola covered her mouth as she swallowed. "I talked to her today in trig, and she's so bummed. She really wanted to compete. This is like her favorite event."

"I know; it's the only one she'll ever compete in because it's not all cutthroat. Jeez, I can't even believe how her parents are reacting. It's like tough love over there for weeks now. But I guess my dad totally surprised me, too, by being so nice about it. Too bad it didn't last." She shrugged.

"Yeah." Lola nodded. Then looking up, she said, "Hey, isn't that Chris?"

"Oh no, where?" Ellie said, sounding totally panicked.

"Directly in front of us. Hey! Chris!" Lola called, waving her arms so he'd see them.

"Why'd you do that? Now he's gonna come over," Ellie whined, shaking her head at Lola.

"What's the big deal?" Lola gave her a strange look.

"I saw him after school today with Anne, and I'm not proud of it, but I was a total bitch to her. So I'm sure he's not very happy with me right now. I was really hoping I could avoid him for a while," Ellie said.

"Well, too late for that. He's headed right for us."

"Hey," Chris said, walking up and smiling. "Have you guys seen Anne?"

Lola shook her head, while Ellie just sat there, staring at the ground.

"I've been trying to reach her but I can't get ahold of her. So I thought I'd drop by and see if I could find her here," he said, shaking his head and looking around.

"Well, if nothing else, she should stop by to register. Why don't you just hang with us until she shows?" Lola said, scooting over and making room between herself and Ellie.

Ellie watched him smile and squeeze in next to her. He didn't seem upset or anything, but she was sure all that would change once Anne showed up.

chapter fifty-seven

Anne climbed out of the Mercedes and looked at Jake. "Just wait here. This should only take a second," she said, anxious to get signed up quickly so they could make it to the restaurant on time.

"Sorry, but I'm coming with," he said, pocketing the keys and following behind her. "Partly because you have no idea where you're going, and partly because this place is packed with babes."

"Fine," she said, rolling her eyes at him. "Just don't get distracted, okay? We're in a hurry."

"Just don't forget who's holding the keys," he said, jangling them for her benefit.

She shook her head and pushed through the crowd. Jake was *so* annoying, and if her dad had just let her drive, then she wouldn't be stuck with him now. *And now he is gonna make a fool of himself by gawking at a bunch of girls who want nothing to do with him*, she thought, spotting the registration table and making a beeline for it.

The second she was finished filling out all the necessary forms and paying the entry fee, she went hunting for

Jake. *Of course he's not where he said he'd be,* she thought, glancing at her watch and making her way through the crowd of people, finally spotting him in the middle of a group of girls, laughing and talking and eating a fish taco.

We're about to have dinner at one of the best restaurants in Laguna Beach and he's eating a taco, she thought, shaking her head and wondering what those girls could possibly see in him. "Jake, sorry, but we've only got fifteen minutes 'til we have to be there," she said, looking from the girls to him and then back again.

He looked at Anne, nodding impatiently. And then to the girls he said, "So I'll see you ladies tomorrow."

"Bye, Jake," they sang, as Anne grabbed his arm and pulled him toward the car.

"You have really bad timing," he told her, following reluctantly.

"And you are so *not* coming tomorrow," she said, still dragging him along.

"And why not?" he asked.

"Because I don't want you watching me." She turned and gave him an annoyed look.

"Well, I hate to break it to you, but I'm not coming for *you.* Those girls invited me."

They did? Could that possibly be true? Anne wondered, feeling her stomach go all weird at the thought. "Oh. Well. Fine," she said, feeling totally embarrassed for assuming he'd want to watch her flail about in the water.

"Hey, isn't that your boyfriend?" Jake stopped just short of the car and pointed.

Anne's eyes followed the direction of his finger. And sure enough, there was Chris, sitting smack in the middle of Lola and Ellie, laughing and looking as though he was having a great time. Maybe even too good of a time.

"Hmmm," Anne mumbled, forcing herself to look away.

"Wanna say a quick hello?" he asked, already starting to head toward them.

But no way was Anne joining *that* little party. "We don't have time," she said, racing toward the car. "We really need to get out of here."

chapter fifty-eight

The morning of Surf Fest, Jade woke up really early feeling really depressed. Well, as depressed as someone who's eternally happy and optimistic can get. Being on restriction the last couple weeks had been bad enough. But missing out on her favorite weekend of the year was an all-new low.

Last night, when she was having dinner with her parents, she was positive they would relent and finally set her free. Especially after she'd cleared her throat, and said, "Tonight's the registration party at San O, and tomorrow's the junior competition." She'd even said it casually, between bites of food, so it would look like she didn't care all that much about it, thinking for sure her parents would look up and say, "Oh, we forgot all about it. Let's clean up this mess and go get you registered!" But her father just nodded and her mom just continued eating, and Jade sat there wondering if this particular punishment would ever end. Yet she didn't dare ask. She was far too terrified of what the answer might be.

Rolling over, she looked out the window next to her bed. The day was just starting to break, which meant people were already arriving, setting up the tents, and getting the coffee and hot chocolate ready to brew. *There has to be a way I can get there with-*

out my parents knowing, she thought. Saturdays were usually pretty busy days for them, with all the beach cleanups and gallery openings they participated in, so they usually weren't around all that much. And if she timed it just right, maybe she'd be able to sneak out just long enough to see Ellie and Anne surf, cheer them on, and then get back home before her parents returned.

Climbing out of bed, she padded into the kitchen and headed straight for the coffeemaker. "You're up early," her dad said, totally startling her.

"Well, today's Surf Fest." She shrugged. "So I guess I'm used to getting up early on this particular day. Even though it's obviously not necessary this year. You know, since you're not letting me compete and all," she said, giving him a sideways glance, trying to gage his reaction.

"Come here," he said, motioning for her to join him at the kitchen table. "We need to talk."

Reluctantly, she pulled out the chair across from him and plopped herself onto it. Then she just sat there, waiting for him to begin.

"I know you're feeling really victimized by your mother and me right now. You probably think we're acting like a bunch of uptight hard-asses. Am I right?"

Jade just shrugged, squirming under his heavy gaze. *Jeez,* it was like he could read her mind or something. Because that's exactly what she had been thinking.

"Well, maybe you're right. But you have no idea what it's like to get a call in the middle of the night from the police station telling you to come pick up your daughter. It's every parent's worst nightmare."

"I know, I know, but I was *fine.* I mean, I did *nothing* wrong. If anything, I was just trying to help Ben," she said, sitting up a little straighter and feeling really virtuous.

"And that's another thing," he said, ominously.

"What?" she asked, pushing her curls out of her eyes, bracing herself for whatever came next.

"Ben." He shook his head. "He's a very troubled young man, and your mother and I prefer you don't have anything more to do with him." He looked right at her.

Jade looked down at the table, running her index finger along the wood grain. "Well, first of all, you don't have to worry about that, since he's living with his dad in Venice Beach. And second, I just don't get it. I mean, you and Mom always act so laid-back and nonjudgmental, not to mention how many of *your* friends you've taken in and helped. But now I try to help just one person who really needs it, and I get punished for my efforts. So, just try and explain *that*," she said, crossing her arms against her chest and looking at him.

"Honey, the difference is that Ben didn't exactly want your help," her dad said, reaching across the table and grabbing her hand. "He was more interested in finding someone to drag down with him. And I'm afraid that you, with your trusting nature and good intentions, were an easy target."

"Thanks a lot," she said, shaking her head and rolling her eyes. *He has no idea what he is talking about. He so doesn't get it.*

"I know you think I don't understand your friendship, but really, I do. And as your dad, I have to tell you it was very troubling to watch. That guy had no regard for your safety, and he put you in a very bad position."

"It was just a little pot." She shrugged.

"Jade, this was not the first time Ben was arrested. A couple weeks ago, he was busted for vandalism. He's in serious trouble now." He looked at her.

Oh my God, that must be why he disappeared for that whole week, she thought, staring at the table again, feeling way too nervous now to look at her dad.

"You need to know that every time we've taken someone in, it was because they *asked* for help. There were never any drugs involved, and there was never any danger posed to you or your sisters. Do you see the difference?"

Finally she looked up at him, nodding slowly. "Okay," she said. "I get it."

"Besides, I don't think we'll be having many more couch crashers in here."

"What do you mean?" she said, eyeing her dad carefully.

"Your mother and I have been talking." He hesitated. "And we're thinking about selling."

"And leave Laguna Cove? But why?" Jade looked at her father in shock. "We love it here."

"The value of this house has more than tripled, and selling it now could allow us to get out of debt and start over."

"But start over *where*? I mean, where would we go? I can't change schools! I don't want to leave my friends!" she said, her voice sounding every bit as frantic as she was feeling.

"Honey, I didn't mean to upset you. We haven't made any final decisions yet, but I want you to know it's a real possibility. It's definitely something we're considering. My last few big pieces haven't done well, you know that, right?"

"But who's to say your next one won't?" Jade said. Then feeling her eyes wet with tears, she got up and went over to the coffeemaker, grabbing the pot and heading for the sink to fill it with water.

"What are you doing?" he asked.

Afraid she'd start crying if she tried to speak, she just held up the pot.

"Put it away, and go get dressed. I figure we can grab some lattes on our way down to San O and that contest." He smiled.

chapter fifty-nine

Ellie was surprised to see her brother knocking on her passenger window. "Hey, let me in," he said.

"What are you doing?" she asked, unlocking the door and giving him a strange look. He'd never wanted to go with her before.

"I'm coming with," he told her, gently laying his video equipment on the backseat and crawling in next to her.

"Why?" she asked, watching him get settled in.

"Car's in the shop." He shrugged.

"But you'll be stuck there all day, totally stranded. I plan on advancing through to the last heat, you know."

"Not a problem. I'll be busy filming. Is Dad gonna make it?" he asked.

Ellie shook her head as she backed out of the driveway and onto the street. "He's already at the hospital," she told him, feeling kind of relieved that her father wouldn't be there to judge her if she choked, but also kind of upset that he wouldn't be there to see her if she won.

"Are any of your friends competing?" he asked, sounding a little too casual while his eyes remained fixed on the road in front of them.

"Jade's still under house arrest. And Lola has cotillion, not to mention that she's not all that into surfing anymore." Ellie shrugged and gave her brother a strange look. *Since when does he care about my friends and their activities?*

"Yeah, I guess her new boyfriend doesn't seem like much of an athlete." He stared out the window.

"Yeah, I guess not," Ellie said, wondering what was up with him as she merged onto the freeway.

chapter sixty

"Lola, are you still asleep?" her mother asked, sticking her head into her room while *Abuela* stood right behind her.

"Not anymore," she said, opening one eye to peer at them and then rolling over to face the wall.

"We have a lot to do today, so I need you to come eat some breakfast so we can get going," her mother said impatiently.

"I made you some eggs and bacon," *Abuela* said, coming over to shake her granddaughter's shoulder.

But Lola just lay there with her eyes closed, slowly counting to ten. She promised herself she would open them the second she reached that number. But she made no promises about how long it might take to get there.

"Get up!" she heard her mother say, in the shrillest voice possible.

Lola rolled over to see *Abuela* smiling down at her, while her mother listed all the very important things that had to be accomplished before this evening's cotillion. "We have to be at the spa in an hour. I've booked us manicures, pedicures, massages, and a hair appointment."

"But I don't want a haircut," Lola said, touching her long, dark hair protectively.

"It's not for a cut. It's for an updo," she told her, while glancing impatiently at her watch. "Now come on. We've got a long day ahead of us and we need to get started right away."

"I'll be there in a minute," Lola said, watching as they left her room and then glancing at the time on her clock radio. *Great. Ellie is going to be surfing her first heat in less than an hour, and there is no way I can get out of this.* Shaking her head in surrender, she stuck her feet in her slippers and walked down the long hallway toward the smell of bacon.

chapter sixty-one

Ellie looked around nervously. She recognized a few people from last year, and everyone seemed to be having so much fun, laughing and joking, as though they had showed up merely for the camaraderie instead of the trophy. But Ellie was here to win, which made her far too nervous to sit around and chat. Last year had ended in disaster, with her getting completely worked by a wave that, if she hadn't been so nervous, she could have handled. And the worst thing was that her father had been standing right there on the shoreline, witnessing every lousy second. So this year she had a lot to prove, but she felt physically and mentally ready to do it. Too bad her dad was gonna miss it.

She kneeled over her board, rubbing it with wax. It was also too bad that Lola and Jade couldn't make it; it just didn't seem the same without them. She knew Anne was already here, having seen her briefly in the parking lot, though they seemed to have a silent agreement to just ignore each other.

Still, it was weird that Anne had shown up alone. Ellie thought for sure Chris would be right there with her. But then again, he hadn't been with her at all last night, since he'd spent the whole time hanging with her and Lola. *Maybe things aren't so great between them after all,* she thought.

"Hey, want some hot chocolate?"

Ellie looked up to see Chris standing there with two steaming cups, smiling at her.

"Oh, I'd love some," she said, reaching for the warm cup.

"What time are you up?" he asked.

"Nine fifteen," she said. And then looking at her watch, "In about ten minutes."

"Are you nervous?" he asked.

"Petrified." She smiled.

"Don't be. You're an amazing surfer, Ellie. And I have no doubt that someday soon you'll be sitting over there." He pointed to the tent where all the sponsored girls were.

Ellie looked over and shrugged. That was her dream. Those girls were the cream of the crop. Talented, gorgeous, athletic, and smart—she longed to be one of them.

"I should head out," she said, finishing her hot chocolate.

"Good luck." He smiled and leaned in to hug her.

"Thanks," Ellie said, closing her eyes and leaning into him, allowing herself to enjoy the closeness, if only for a moment.

But just as she pulled away she opened her eyes and saw Anne, not more than six feet away, standing there watching them.

chapter sixty-two

Anne was bent over her board, furiously waxing it, trying to make sense of what she just witnessed. That was the second time in less than twenty-four hours that she'd seen Chris and Ellie together, and she was absolutely positive that it was not a coincidence that both those events just happened to take place after she foolishly told him all about Ellie being in love with him.

Well, that's what you get, she thought. *You practically threw him in her path.* And why wouldn't he like Ellie? Other than being a total bitch (and what guy ever cared about that?), Ellie had it all—she was beautiful, brainy, popular, rich, a great surfer, not to mention how she and Chris went way back. And there was just no way Anne could compete with that. Hadn't she already learned that lesson when Justin dumped her for Vanessa?

Picking up her board, she headed toward the water, stopping to watch Ellie paddling around and maneuvering into the best position possible. *If Ellie is a shark, then I'm her dinner,* she thought. *And I'll surely be eaten alive.*

chapter sixty-three

Ellie had only fifteen minutes to be scored on ten waves, with the bottom seven numbers being thrown out. But Ellie was determined to surf all ten waves amazingly well. There would be no throwaways as far as she was concerned.

While the other girls around her laughed and talked, Ellie kept to herself, watching the waves and devising a strategy. She'd watched Anne paddle out, looking completely lost and unsure of what to do next, but Ellie just shrugged it off. That was Anne's problem. Ellie wasn't here to baby-sit some newbie. She had a contest to win.

When the moment felt exactly right, she started paddling, and then hopping onto her board, she rode the wave confidently and carefully all the way to the shore. *But maybe I've been just a little too careful,* she thought as she turned around to head back out. She hadn't done anything remotely impressive, but then again, at least she hadn't choked.

Lying on her board, she paddled quickly toward the break. She had nine more waves to go, and no time to spare.

chapter sixty-four

Anne was totally lost. Some of the girls who seemed so nice and helpful just a moment ago were now totally focused on their own performance, and she was left wondering just what the hell she'd been thinking to even attempt this in the first place. She'd been surfing now, for what, a month? It was totally ridiculous of her to think she could pull this off. Especially after watching Ellie's awesome performance.

Ellie had just surfed her sixth wave and she was totally carving it up out there. There was no doubt that she would be advancing to the next heat, while Anne would probably be free to go home sometime within the next ten minutes.

She tried to remember her diving days, when she had been the one to beat, just like Ellie was now. But it didn't exactly compare, since she'd been diving since she was eight, and everything was just so much easier back then, mostly because people were pretty impressed with just about anything you did at that age. But now, at almost seventeen, the pressure was much greater, especially when she knew Ellie was out there like a vulture, patiently watching and waiting for her to fail.

Oh well. It beats wearing an ugly bridesmaid's dress at your pregnant mom's shotgun wedding, she thought, popping up on her board, determined to at least make it to shore without falling off.

chapter sixty-five

Lola's nails were wet, her face was caked with make-up, and her hair was all piled up high on top of her head like a big chocolate-frosted cake. "I'm supposed to walk around like this *all day*?" she asked, shuddering at her own reflection. She looked more like a Vegas showgirl than a virginal debutante about to be introduced to society.

"Well, it's not like we're going anywhere else. After here it's just home, until it's time to put on your dress and go," her mother told her.

"Uh, wrong," Lola said, shaking her head carefully so as not to dislodge the million bobby pins and sparkly barrettes that were holding the whole mess together. "I told Diego I'd meet him." She nodded, having come up with this genius excuse sometime between the massage and the body scrub.

"You are not meeting Diego," her mom said, turning away from the increasingly frustrated makeup artist. "You will see him tonight at cotillion. You two are just gonna have to wait until then."

Lola noticed the little smile on her mom's face when she said that, like she was so proud of herself for introducing her daughter to her future husband. *If she only knew,* Lola thought, shaking her head. "Mom, it can't wait. Because he wants to give me . . . " She hesitated; she hadn't really thought it all the way through to this point. ". . . a present. He has a present for me that he wants me to have . . . for tonight," she concluded, thinking how now she'd also have to stop by the mall to pick up some little trinket and then pretend it was from Diego. She'd have to make sure she wore her sunglasses, 'cause there was no way she could be seen lurking around South Coast Plaza with hair like this.

"Fine," her mother said, frowning as Lola jumped up from her chair. "But be home as quickly as possible. Your hair and makeup have to last until tonight, you know."

"Don't worry," Lola said, slipping her flip-flops onto her feet and thinking how odd she must look with her California girl clothes and Spanish soap opera hair and makeup.

chapter sixty-six

Anne could not believe when she heard her name called. "Third place," Jake said, smiling and slapping her on the back. "That means you get to go on to the next heat!"

"It does? Are you serious?" she asked. The scoring and rules were all new to her, so she sincerely hoped he wasn't just fooling around.

"Yeah, but it doesn't start for a while, so you can just chill," he said, smiling.

"Did you hear that?" she said, as her dad and Brooke approached. "I'm advancing to the next heat. I mean, I'll probably choke on that one, but I don't even care! It just feels so awesome to get to this point!" She was so excited, she even hugged Brooke.

"I just saw Chris," her father said. "He's looking for you. I told him you were over here."

"Oh, really?" Anne bit down on her lip, wondering why Chris was looking for her. Was he going to break up with her? Right now? Well, he'd just have to wait, since there was no way she was going to let him ruin her day. The last thing she needed was for some stupid relationship drama to kill her buzz, and there was no way she was gonna let him bring her down. "Well, if he comes by, just tell him I'll catch up with him later. I'm totally starving. I'm gonna grab something to eat." And then, grabbing Jake by the arm, she said, "Wanna join me?"

chapter sixty-seven

Ellie wasn't surprised she'd advanced to the second heat. Nor was she surprised that she came in first. But what did surprise her was the sight of Lola walking across the beach with the biggest hair she'd ever seen.

"Don't even mention it," Lola said, holding up her hand defensively. "In fact, please don't even look at it."

"How can I not?" Ellie said, laughing. "It's huge!'

"Can you even believe it?" She rolled her eyes. "I swear, the things Lola will do to please her mother . . ."

"And the things Lolita will do to be a good friend," Ellie said, hugging her gently so as not to get stabbed in the eye by a pink heart-shaped rhinestone barrette. "I can't believe you showed up."

"Hey, I haven't missed one of these yet. And for your information, Jade's here, too. I just saw her with her dad; they were talking to Chris."

"Is she surfing?" Ellie asked.

"No. Apparently, she had to learn a lesson about the consequences of certain actions, or however her dad phrased it." She rolled her eyes.

"Well, how long are you staying?" Ellie asked.

"Long enough to totally embarrass myself with this updo, and see you nail a trophy and a sponsorship." She smiled.

chapter sixty-eight

"So why are you using me to hide from your boy-friend?" Jake asked, taking a sip of his coffee and looking right at Anne.

"Don't be ridiculous," she said, feeling her face go every shade of fuchsia. "I don't even know what you're talking about." She shook her head and sipped her drink, avoiding his eyes.

"The dude's been looking all over for you, but you keep hiding—mostly behind me. So, what's the deal? You guys in a fight?" he asked.

"I . . ." Anne hesitated, feeling frustrated because she really didn't know how to answer. Because she really didn't know what the answer was. "I'd really rather not talk about it, if you don't mind," she said, placing her hands on her hips and narrowing her eyes at him.

"Okay, that's cool," he said, looking at her and nodding. "You know you're gonna be a real catch someday—when you grow up." He smiled.

"What's that supposed to mean?" she asked.

But he just looked at her, tossed his empty coffee cup in the bin, and started to walk away.

"For your information, you're only two years older than me!"

she yelled after him, feeling even more annoyed when he just smiled, waved, and kept walking.

Oh, that's just great, she thought, standing there and staring after him as he weaved his way through the crowd of people. *Who does he think he is, talking to me like that? He works for my dad! And he should really learn to be more respectful.* He had no idea what was going on in her life, and he had no right to judge her.

She shook her head and looked out at the water. Thirty more minutes until her next heat, and there was no way she was gonna let Jake upset her. *He is nothing to me. He's just a minor annoyance,* she told herself as she headed back toward her surfboard.

chapter sixty-nine

Lola sat on the shoreline with Jade, trying to forget about her stupid hair and the fact that everyone who walked past her turned and did a double take. Ellie and Anne were out there surfing, and even though on the surface she was rooting for them both, deep down inside she really wanted Ellie to win, mostly because she had the most riding on it.

"I wish I was out there," Jade said. "I really blew it this time."

"There's always next year." Lola shrugged.

But Jade knew that wasn't necessarily true. Feeling her eyes start to sting with tears, she closed them until the moment passed. She wished she could confide in Lola about her conversation with her dad—about how they might have to leave Laguna Cove and move far away. But she was barely able to admit it to herself, much less her best friends. So, determined to put it out of her mind, she decided not to say anything.

"Who knows, maybe I'll even enter it with you." Lola laughed, but her smile froze into place when she spotted Dean standing just a few feet away. And he was looking right at her.

"Oh my God," Jade said. "I think Anne's going for it. Oh, I can't look. It makes me too nervous. I'm gonna go pee instead." She got up from her towel.

"Now?" Lola asked, panicked. The last thing she needed was to be left alone. Because then Dean might come over. And she had no idea what she'd say to him if that happened.

"Yeah, I'll be right back." Jade gave her a strange look.

"But can't you wait?" Lola asked, realizing how needy and ridiculous she sounded. But there's no way she could let Jade leave her.

"What's the deal?" Jade said, hopping anxiously from one foot to the other.

"Nothing." Lola shook her head with resignation. "Go ahead."

Jade ran off toward the bathrooms while Lola looked out at the ocean. Anne had just fallen off her board. *That's gotta hurt,* she thought, cringing as she watched Anne get worked by a wave.

"Hey."

Lola knew the voice, so she was reluctant to look up and actually see the person it belonged to. "Hey," she said, her eyes remaining focused on the ocean in front of her, since she didn't know how to face Dean.

"How've you been?" he asked, kneeling down next to her.

"Okay." She shrugged. Then, suddenly remembering her outrageous hair and makeup, she began to feel really self-conscious. "You're not filming me, are you?" she asked, glancing nervously at his camera.

"Um, no," he said, turning it away from her and putting the lens cap back on. "Listen, Lola, I don't really know how to say this, and you know I'm not that good with words and stuff, but I miss you." He gave her a tentative, shy look.

"You do?" She turned toward him, her eyes going wide. *Could he possibly really mean that?*

"Yeah." He blushed. "But I know you have a new boyfriend now, and you guys seem really happy, so I'm not looking for anything. I just wanted to apologize for ending everything so abruptly. I can see now that I made a big mistake."

Lola just looked at him. After all this time, after all the heartache she'd endured, he'd finally just said all the right things, using all the right words. And now she had a choice. She could either tell him the truth about Diego and end the whole stupid charade right now, or she could keep her secret and let Dean suffer just a little while longer.

She looked right into his eyes and slowly trailed a finger down his cheek. "I really appreciate you saying that." She smiled. "And I really hope that we can still be friends."

chapter seventy

Ellie had one more wave to go and plenty of time in which to do it. She was on fire today, having never surfed better in her life. But Anne had just wiped out again, and Ellie noticed that her face was all red as she paddled back in. There was no way she would make it to the final heat. She'd had a decent enough start, but now she was totally falling apart. And even if she did surf a perfect last wave, it still wouldn't be enough. It was pretty much over for her.

Ellie saw Anne glance at her warily and then position herself as far from her as possible. Which also just happened to be the absolute worst place she could have picked. And it made Ellie wonder if Anne chose it because she had no idea how bad it was, or if she chose it so she could be far away from Ellie.

Oh my God, what have I done, she thought. *I've turned into such a jealous, competitive, nasty bitch that I'm actually sabotaging this poor girl's chances! And isn't that like, the exact opposite of what surfing is supposed to be about?*

Ellie looked at her watch—she had two minutes left to catch her last wave and really shred it to impress the judges.

Or she could help someone who really needed it.

chapter seventy-one

Anne sat on her board, choking back tears and hoping that the salt water pouring from her eyes was blending in with the salt water from the ocean, so no one would know what a big, pathetic baby she was being. What had started out as a pretty good day had quickly gone to hell. She felt bad about her mom's wedding, she felt bad about Chris avoiding her (or was she avoiding Chris?), and she felt inexplicably bad about Jake's stupid little comment.

Even her surfing had fallen apart, and her body felt bruised and battered from getting worked by so many waves. And now, to just top off this miserable day, that total bitch, Ellie, was sitting on her board waving at her. God, she was like a pit bull. She just never let up.

Oh well, I may as well get the last wave out of the way, she thought. *I mean, I have to get back to shore somehow.* Anne started to paddle, but stopped when Ellie charged right in front of her. "What do you want?" Anne glared at her.

"I want to help you, if you'll let me," Ellie told her.

"Yeah, right. You probably came all the way over here just to gloat. Well fine, you're winning, *okay?* You're winning at ab-solutely everything. You're taking Surf Fest, you're taking Chris, and now you probably want to take me down. Am I right?" Anne looked away. There was no way she would cry in front of her.

"Listen, we don't have a lot of time," Ellie said. "And you're right, I'm ahead and you're not. But it really doesn't matter anymore. I mean, don't you want to surf one really awesome wave before you go home?"

Anne just looked at her, not sure if this was for real or not.

"I can help you do that, if you'll just follow me. Oh, and for the record," Ellie said, turning back to look at her. "Chris likes *you*, not *me*. And I'm okay with that."

chapter seventy-two

"Oh my God, look at her! I think she's really gonna take it this year!" Chris said, grabbing Anne's hand and watching Ellie surf her very last wave of the junior's final heat.

"Oh, I can't look," Jade said, covering her eyes. "Just, just give me a play-by-play but don't tell me if she falls, 'cause I don't want to know about it."

"You're just gonna have to open your eyes and see it for yourself because the girl is *rippin' it up*," Lola said, glancing back and forth between Ellie out in the water and Dean running up and down the shoreline taping her.

"Hey, don't you have cotillion?" Anne asked.

"Yeah, but I'm not budging 'til this is all said and done," Lola said, glancing briefly at Anne, and then back at the water. "Oh my God, she made it. She did it! *Yes!*" Lola got up from her towel, and jumped up and down on the sand, while bobby pins and barrettes sprang from her hair, landing all around her.

"Uh, Lola, I think your hair just popped," Jade said, pointing at Lola's sunken updo and laughing.

"Oh, who cares?" Lola yanked out the remaining bobby pins and barrettes and threw them onto her towel. Then, quickly combing her fingers through her long, dark hair, she ran down to the water, toward Dean.

chapter seventy-three

"You did it! You were *amazing!*" Jade said hugging Ellie, while Chris and Anne nodded in agreement.

"You think so?" Ellie asked, squeezing the salt water from her hair. "I mean, you never know until the scores are read, right?"

"You totally deserve to win," Anne said, looking at her and smiling.

Ellie smiled back; then looking past Anne she noticed Duncan standing just a few feet away, with his arm around a pretty brunette who she had just competed against. Their eyes met briefly, and Duncan smiled and waved. But Ellie just nodded, surprised by the way she felt at seeing him with another girl.

"Honey, there's someone waiting to talk to you," her dad said, interrupting her train of thought.

"Dad! You made it! Did you see me?" Ellie asked, feeling like a little kid begging, *Look at me, Daddy! Look at me!*

"I didn't get here 'til your final heat, but I saw all of it. You were amazing." He smiled and hugged her tight. "I'm so proud of you," he whispered.

Ellie clung to him until the threat of tears had passed, and then she pulled away and said, "So who wants to talk to me?"

"Some surf-brand big shot," he said, looking at her and smiling. "He mentioned something about a sponsorship?"

Ellie grabbed her dad's hand and headed toward the tent. Her biggest dream was about to come true, but the thing that she felt the most proud of was something the sponsors and judges never even saw. But she knew. And Anne knew. And maybe, in some strange way, even her mom knew.

Stopping for a moment, she lifted her face toward the sun, closing her eyes and feeling the warmth against her skin. Then, looking over at her father, she smiled and squeezed his hand as they continued toward the tent.